THE DEMON HEADMASTER TAKES OVER

Also by Gillian Cross

The Demon Headmaster
The Demon Headmaster and the Prime Minister's Brain
The Revenge of the Demon Headmaster
The Demon Headmaster Strikes Again
Facing the Demon Headmaster

The Tree House

FOR OLDER READERS
'The Lost' Trilogy
The Dark Ground
The Black Room
The Nightmare Game

A Map of Nowhere
Born of the Sun
Calling a Dead Man
Chartbreak
On the Edge
Pictures in the Dark
Roscoe's Leap
The Dark Behind the Curtain
The Great Elephant Chase
The Iron Way
Tightrope
Where I Belong
Wolf

THE DEMON HEADMASTER TAKES OVER

gillian cross

OXFORD
UNIVERSITY PRESS

OXFORD
UNIVERSITY PRESS

Great Clarendon Street, Oxford OX2 6DP

Oxford University Press is a department of the University of Oxford.
It furthers the University's objective of excellence in research, scholarship,
and education by publishing worldwide in

Oxford New York

Auckland Cape Town Dar es Salaam Hong Kong Karachi
Kuala Lumpur Madrid Melbourne Mexico City Nairobi
New Delhi Shanghai Taipei Toronto

With offices in

Argentina Austria Brazil Chile Czech Republic France Greece
Guatemala Hungary Italy Japan Poland Portugal Singapore
South Korea Switzerland Thailand Turkey Ukraine Vietnam

Oxford is a registered trade mark of Oxford University Press
in the UK and in certain other countries

First published in this edition 2010

2

British Library Cataloguing in Publication Data

Data available

ISBN: 978-019-275586-5

Printed in Great Britain by Clays Ltd, St Ives plc
Paper used in the production of this book is a natural,
recyclable product made from wood grown in sustainable forests.
The manufacturing process conforms to the environmental
regulations of the country of origin.

1

Switched on Again

'It's the army!'

'What?' Dinah Hunter blinked and rubbed her eyes. Her younger brother, Harvey, was standing in the doorway. 'Are you mad?' she said. 'It's the middle of the night.'

'But the army's here!' Harvey ran across the room. He was holding a pair of binoculars, and he pushed them at her. 'They're opening up the Research Centre!'

'*What?*' Dinah sat up. 'Don't be silly, Harvey.'

'I'm not being silly. You can see them clearing the doorways. And look at the lights!'

'The lights? You mean they've turned the electricity on?' Dinah grabbed the binoculars and jumped out of bed.

The Research Centre was on the other side of the village, but she could see it over the roofs of the houses. For months it had been closed and sealed up, a dark, silent building gradually disappearing under layers of creeper.

Now the windows were blazing with light. Through the binoculars, Dinah could see vehicles pulled up all round the building. There were shadowy figures too, hacking at the creeper with machetes. One of the figures walked through a spotlight beam and she saw his army uniform.

'What are they up to?' she muttered.

'They're trying to get in,' Harvey whispered. 'Maybe they know—'

He was speaking softly, but not softly enough. Suddenly, their mother shouted up the stairs.

'Harvey? Dinah? Are you *talking*?'

'Sorry, Mum,' Dinah called. 'We're just—'

'I don't care what you're doing.' Mrs Hunter sounded tired. 'Go to sleep. The removal men are coming at half-past eight tomorrow and they'll expect us to be up.'

'That's right.' Their father joined in. 'Whatever you're discussing, it can wait until tomorrow.'

Dinah shrugged and handed the binoculars back to Harvey. 'He's right,' she whispered. 'We can't do anything tonight. Go back to sleep.'

Harvey hesitated for a second, frowning at the Research Centre. Then he padded back to his room. Dinah sighed and climbed back into bed, snuggling under her duvet. In a few moments, she was asleep.

But it wasn't a peaceful sleep . . .

She dreamt she was inside the Research Centre

8

again, standing in front of a huge computer. Lights flashed on the control panels and words flicked on and off the screen, but she hardly noticed them. Her eyes were fixed on the black hole that gaped below the screen like a great, greedy mouth.

Something moved inside the hole. Something long and pale, that scrabbled at the sides, hunting for a place to grip.

A hand.

Its fingers closed round the rim of the hole, clamping tight, and another hand began struggling out of the darkness.

On the screen above, there were bright red letters flashing on the screen.

EVOLUTION ACCELERATOR ACTIVATED
DNA REPRODUCED

The hands tightened, pulling on the edges of the hole, and slowly a head emerged. A man's head, with a stern, pale face and strange, sea-green eyes . . .

'No!' Dinah shouted. 'No!'

The thin lips opened soundlessly, mouthing words that hung in the air. *You are feeling very sleepy* . . .

'No!'

Dinah woke with a jolt. Slowly she sat up and looked across the room.

Now that it was light, she could see the Research Centre even more clearly. The soldiers must have been working all night. Yesterday, its walls had been green with creeper. Now they were half bare.

Sliding out of bed, Dinah went to take a closer look. There was still creeper growing over the top of the building, and snaking out from inside, but the soldiers had cleared a huge amount. There was a big stack of broken stems in the car park.

As she watched, one of the men picked up a flame-thrower and aimed it at the stack. A jet of fire shot out and the huge green heap shrivelled into a little pile of smoking ash.

One flame. That was all it took.

The scientists at the Research Centre had used all their skill and knowledge to produce that creeper. They had studied the structure of DNA. They'd learnt how to manipulate it. They'd designed a machine that could reproduce the new DNA. *And the army's going to wipe it all out in a single day*, Dinah thought.

She couldn't just stand by and see it all vanish.

Picking up her jeans, she felt in the pockets and found her little notebook. She leafed through the pages, until she came to the name and address she wanted.

Professor Claudia Rowe
Biological Sciences Department
University of Wessex.

Underneath was the telephone number. She hadn't thought she would ever need that, but maybe she did now. The soldiers were destroying the creeper very fast.

'They're doing *what?*' Professor Rowe shrieked down the phone.

Dinah had to shout too. The removal men had arrived, and it was very noisy. 'They've already cut quite a lot.' She stepped out of the way as two men came past with her bed. 'They're burning it.'

'But it's unique!' Professor Rowe sounded horrified. 'There's nothing like it, anywhere else in the world. *You* know that, Dinah.'

Dinah knew all right. She knew more than Professor Rowe. She'd been in the lab where the creeper was made—and seen the Evolution Accelerator that had made it. 'But what can I do?' she said.

Professor Rowe was thinking out loud. 'We must get hold of some samples, before it's too late. You'll have to go down there and talk to them, Dinah.'

'Me?'

'There's no one else. I'll set out straight away, but it'll take me at least an hour. You've got to stall them until I get there. Plead. Threaten them with a scandal. Do whatever it takes—but don't let them destroy that creeper!'

'But—'

But we're moving, Dinah was going to say. Professor Rowe didn't give her a chance.

'Once they destroy that creeper, we've lost it for ever!' she said fiercely. 'They're destroying *knowledge*, and knowledge is precious. Go and fight for it, Dinah! I'll be there as soon as I can.'

She rang off, and Dinah put down the phone and took a deep breath. She'd have to go. She hated the sight of the creeper, but Professor Rowe was right. Knowledge was precious.

She called down the hall. 'I'm just going out for a bit.'

'Are you mad?' Lloyd, her other brother, stuck his head out of the kitchen. 'You can't go out now.'

'I've got to,' Dinah said stubbornly. 'I'm going to the Research Centre.'

'To see the army?' Eagerly, Harvey came rattling down the stairs. 'I'll come too!'

Mrs Hunter ran out of her bedroom with an armful of bedding. 'Dinah, you can't—'

'It's important,' Dinah said quietly.

12

'To go and look at a lot of soldiers?' Lloyd looked scornful. 'You're like a couple of two year olds.'

But Mrs Hunter was watching Dinah's face. 'Really important?' she said.

Dinah nodded.

'All right. You can go. But don't be long.'

'Thanks, Mum.' Dinah snatched up her coat and headed out of the house. Lloyd turned away in disgust, but Harvey was right behind her.

The road outside the Research Centre was crowded with villagers. Three soldiers were stationed at the gate, to keep people away from the building. Dinah looked at them and then wriggled through the crowd to Mrs Pritchett from the Post Office. She always knew what was going on.

'What's up, Mrs Pritchett?'

'They're destroying that creeper,' Mrs Pritchett said. 'About time, too. It'll be all over the village next.'

'It's slowed down,' Harvey said. 'It used to grow much faster than that.'

Mrs Pritchett sniffed. 'That's only the season. If they leave it till next spring, it'll be twice as bad. Got to get rid of it now.'

'There's lots inside the building,' Dinah said.

She could see it pressing against the windows. 'Are they going to burn that too?'

Mrs Pritchett shrugged. 'Suppose so. But no one's gone in yet. Except one little fellow in a brown anorak.'

'Perhaps he's in charge,' muttered Harvey.

'Him?' Mrs Pritchett looked scornful. 'No, *that's* the commanding officer. The tall man, by the gate.'

That was the man they needed to speak to, then! Dinah grabbed Harvey's arm.

'Come on.'

Harvey went pale. 'But we can't—'

'Yes we can!' Dinah started pulling him towards the tall soldier. 'You can't burn that creeper!' she shouted. 'You're destroying knowledge!'

Back at the Hunters' house, Mrs Hunter was getting impatient.

'Aren't Dinah and Harvey back yet?'

Lloyd was watching the removal men shut the lorry. He turned round and shrugged. 'Not unless they're hiding.'

Mrs Hunter frowned. 'How can they be so thoughtless!'

Mr Hunter put a hand on her shoulder. 'No problem,' he said. 'Lloyd can go and fetch them

14

back. He's not doing anything useful. Off you go, Lloyd!'

Typical! Why was it always him who had to sort things out? Lloyd sighed and set off, grumbling under his breath.

He was halfway through the village when a white sports car came screeching past. It stopped abruptly and the driver jumped out and called back to him.

'How do I get to the Biogenetic Research Centre?' She was a fairly young woman, in jeans, and she looked fierce and anxious.

'Turn left at the top.' Lloyd pointed. 'You can't miss it—'

Before he could finish, she had jumped back into the car and driven off.

What was the big hurry? Why was everyone obsessed with the Research Centre? The place had been shut down for months and nothing was going to happen there.

By the time he reached the Centre himself, the woman was talking to the soldiers. She was waving her hands about and shouting.

'I'm a biologist, Major Pearce! That creeper is unique. It's already given me crucial ideas for the work I'm doing! If you destroy it, you'll be setting scientific development back for years!'

Dinah was there too. Lloyd couldn't hear what

she said, but her cheeks were pink and she was nodding fiercely. Harvey was just behind her, looking embarrassed.

Major Pearce was obviously trying to be polite. 'I appreciate your concern, but there's important equipment in that building. It must be rescued before the creeper destroys it.'

'What sort of equipment?' the woman said scornfully.

The major avoided her eyes. 'I'm not at liberty to say.'

Lloyd decided it was time he took Harvey and Dinah away. He went marching up to them. 'Come on, you two. We're leaving. Now!'

'Not yet!' Dinah said impatiently. 'Professor Rowe needs me.'

'Professor who?' Lloyd looked round. He was imagining an old man with a mop of white hair.

It was the young woman from the sports car who answered. She stopped shouting at Major Pearce and held out her hand.

'*I'm* Professor Rowe. Call me Claudia.'

'I . . . er . . . hello.' Lloyd let his hand be shaken. 'I'm Lloyd. Dinah's brother.'

'Come to get her?' Claudia said briskly. 'Well, she won't be long. We just need some samples of this creeper. Come on, Dinah!'

Catching hold of Dinah's hand, she side-stepped

16

neatly round the soldiers and began striding towards the Research Centre.

Harvey looked frantically at Lloyd. 'They'll get shot!'

Major Pearce's hand was already sliding inside his jacket, but it wasn't a gun he pulled out. It was a mobile phone. He tapped in a number, very quickly, and began to talk in a low, urgent voice.

'Mr Smith? Major Pearce here. Sorry to trouble you, sir, but we may have a problem.'

Lloyd couldn't make out the answer, but it sounded irritable. Whoever Mr Smith was, he didn't like being disturbed. His voice went on and on and Major Pearce rolled his eyes up to the sky.

'Intelligence!' he muttered, under his breath.

But his voice was polite when he spoke into the phone.

'Yes, sir, I realize you're doing something important in there. Yes, sir. And confidential. But a professor's turned up. She says we can't torch the creeper because it's unique. And she's on her way into the building.'

There was another burst of irritable words.

Major Pearce sighed. 'Yes, I could have stopped her. But she would have caused a lot of trouble. It's Professor Rowe, sir. From Wessex University. Claudia Rowe.'

There was a silence, and then something that

sounded like an order. Major Pearce switched off the phone hastily. Without even glancing at Lloyd and Harvey, he set off after Dinah and Claudia, almost running across the forecourt.

'He's going to arrest them!' Harvey hissed.

But he was wrong. Major Pearce caught up with Claudia and Dinah, said something to them, and led the way towards the doorway the soldiers had cleared. Lloyd watched the three of them disappear inside the building. *Oh great*, he thought crossly. *How am I going to get Dinah now?*

Harvey was watching too. 'Do you think they'll be all right?'

'Of course they'll be all right,' Lloyd snapped. 'Why shouldn't they be?'

'Well, there's . . . there's the Evolution Accelerator,' Harvey mumbled, staring down at his feet. 'You know it can copy people, from their DNA. You don't suppose—?'

Lloyd knew what he was thinking. 'Oh, stop worrying! He's gone. He's never coming back. You all saw him disappear into that hole. The Evolution Accelerator swallowed him up.'

'But what if—?'

'He's *gone*, Harvey.'

2

Who Stole Mr Smith?

Dinah shivered as she walked into the Research Centre again. It felt like going back into a dragon's mouth.

But everything had changed. Last time, the place had been bustling with people, all working hard. Now it was empty, and the corridors were full of creeper.

Claudia was staring round in amazement. 'It's like the Sleeping Beauty's palace in here.'

'Maybe that's what's happened to Mr Smith,' Major Pearce said crossly. 'Perhaps he's turned into the Sleeping Beauty.' He punched at the buttons of his mobile phone again. 'Why isn't he answering?'

'He's not far away,' Dinah said. 'Listen.'

Very faintly, from the far end of the long corridor, they heard another mobile phone ringing.

'What's the point of phoning if he's that close?' Claudia said. 'We can go and see him.'

She began to walk down the corridor, stepping over tangles of creeper and brushing aside the strands that hung down from the ceiling. Major Pearce followed her, but he didn't stop dialling.

Dinah could see that he wanted to warn Mr Smith that they were coming.

When they were halfway down the corridor, the distant ringing stopped.

'Hang on a minute, Professor,' Major Pearce called. He spoke into the phone. 'Mr Smith?'

His voice echoed down the corridor—and back towards them from the other phone.

Mr Smith?

There was no answer.

Major Pearce hesitated, and then tried again. 'Sir? I'm on my way to the lab with Professor Rowe, from the University of Wessex.'

His unanswered voice echoed forlornly in the silence . . . *on my way to the lab with Professor Rowe. From the University of Wessex.*

Claudia was starting to get impatient. 'What's going on? Who is this Mr Smith, anyway?'

Major Pearce looked evasive. 'He's . . . well, it's a little delicate . . . I can't exactly spell out—'

'Oh, he's from Intelligence, is he?' Claudia looked scornful. 'They get everywhere.' Her voice rose, irritably. 'It makes me sick the way Intelligence has all the power. It takes over everything!'

She spoke so loudly that the major's phone picked up her voice. Dinah heard the words coming back from the far end of the corridor.

Intelligence has all the power. It takes over everything!

The major glared at her. 'That's nonsense. I'm the one in charge. I'm just wondering what's become of him.'

'Maybe he's been kidnapped by aliens,' Claudia said drily. 'Let's hope there's a security camera. Then we can watch it all on the video.'

The ghost of her voice echoed from the other phone. *We can watch it all on the video.* The major switched off his own phone and pushed it into his pocket.

'All right,' he said. 'Let's go and see.'

He walked briskly down the corridor ahead of them and pushed at the lab door.

'Hello?'

It took him a few moments to get the door open properly, because there was a thick tangle of creepers behind it. He put his shoulder against the top panel and shoved. Then he waded over the creeper stalks, with Claudia close behind.

As she followed, Dinah glanced up at the ceiling. She spotted the security camera straight away. It was mounted high in one corner, where it would catch the face of everyone who walked into the lab.

It must have filmed her face, last time she was there. And the video had probably not been changed. The past was still there, in pictures.

The idea made her shudder. She stepped further into the lab, feeling as if she'd walked into her dream. She half-expected to hear the Evolution Accelerator humming and clicking, and see that tall, terrible figure facing her across the room. Staring at her with his sea-green eyes . . .

But the lab was empty.

Someone had obviously been there recently, because the creeper that grew across the floor was trampled and bruised, but there was no sign of anyone now. Everything was switched off.

Claudia walked into the middle of the room and stared around. 'There's some pretty strange equipment here. What's *that*, for example?' She nodded at the Evolution Accelerator.

'It's for analysing DNA,' Dinah said. 'And altering it. That's how the creeper was produced.'

'Fascinating!' Claudia's eyes gleamed. 'I suppose the samples went into that hole under the screen.' She walked across and peered into it. Then she glanced sideways. 'What about those headphones?'

'There's some kind of concentrated learning system, I think.' Dinah reached out to pick up the headphones.

'Leave those alone!' the major snapped. 'All this equipment is highly secret.' He looked round the room. 'Is there another way out? What's that door over there?'

'It leads down to the old cellars,' Dinah said. 'And out through the ice house.'

22

Major Pearce strode across to the door and wrenched it open. The three of them stared at the steps that led down into the darkness.

'Mr Smith *could* have gone that way,' Claudia said. 'But why would he bother?'

'Maybe he wasn't on his own,' Major Pearce said grimly.

Claudia gave a snort of laughter. 'You mean someone else got in? With all those soldiers outside?'

The major frowned. 'Of course not!' But he looked worried. 'I think I'd better get that security video.'

Taking out a key, he marched over to a little door in the wall. But when it swung open, he gave a loud grunt. There was nothing behind the door, except an empty space.

'It's gone?' Claudia looked amused. 'Maybe Mr Smith's taken it.'

'Maybe,' the major said. But he looked even more worried.

'I don't think you need to fret.' Claudia shrugged. 'Those Intelligence people can take care of themselves. The creeper's in more danger than he is.'

'Oh yes. The creeper.' The major glanced round absent-mindedly. 'You want to take some samples?'

'Lots,' Claudia said briskly. 'With seed pods if possible.'

'There are some lovely seed pods in the corridor,' said Dinah. 'I'll show you.'

She turned to lead the way and caught her foot in the tangled creeper on the floor. Staggering sideways, she put out a hand to steady herself against the Evolution Accelerator.

It was warm!

Dinah was so startled that she couldn't speak. And before she could collect her thoughts, Major Pearce began to hustle her. He was obviously anxious to get the two of them out of the building.

'Come along. I can't give you very long.'

Claudia was already out in the corridor. With a last backward glance at the Evolution Accelerator, Dinah followed, rubbing her fingers together.

Had she imagined that strange, warm tingle? Or had the Evolution Accelerator been running?

Outside, Lloyd was fuming.

'It's ridiculous! Dinah can't stay in there for ever. We'd better go and get her out!'

'I don't think—' Harvey began timidly.

Lloyd ignored him. Squaring his shoulders, he marched up to the main gate of the Research Centre, as if he were going to walk straight through. But he didn't get very far. The moment he got near, a soldier barred his way.

'Sorry, laddie. It's top secret in there.'

Laddie! Lloyd tried not to look sick. 'I've got to get my sister out. We're leaving here any minute. Moving away.'

The soldier shrugged helplessly. 'Not my fault. I don't make the decisions around here.'

'What's the matter?' Mrs Pritchett called from the other side of the road. She came bustling across to Lloyd. 'Do you need any help, dear?'

Dear! Lloyd forced himself to smile politely. 'We need to get into the Research Centre. To fetch Dinah.'

Mrs Pritchett glared at the soldier. 'Where's the harm in that? You can let the boy in for a moment, can't you?'

'I haven't got the authority,' the soldier said patiently. 'No one except the major or Mr Smith can give permission for people to go in there.'

Lloyd glanced round at the other soldiers. 'OK, then. Which one's Mr Smith? I'll ask him.'

'Oh, he's not in uniform.' The soldier looked amused. 'Wears a sort of shabby brown anorak.'

'The little fellow who went inside earlier on?' Mrs Pritchett said. 'Well, they can't ask him. He drove off about five minutes ago. Though he wasn't fit to be in charge of a car, if you ask me. He looked half asleep.'

'He drove off?' The soldier looked startled. 'But—I thought he was inside.'

25

'Came out the back way and went off in a car.' Mrs Pritchett looked pleased with herself for knowing more than the army. 'That man who used to run the Research Centre was with him. Seemed to be ordering him about.'

Harvey caught his breath. '*What* man who used to run the Research Centre?'

'*You* know,' Mrs Pritchett said. 'That tall man in dark glasses. I haven't seen him around for a while.'

'He's come back?' Harvey said. He went pale and looked at Lloyd.

'It must have been someone else,' Lloyd said quickly. 'Come on, Harvey. We're not going to get into the building. Mum and Dad will have to come and get Dinah out.'

He pulled Harvey away, before he could start talking nonsense. Keeping hold of his arm, he started marching him down the road.

'But it's *him*,' Harvey whispered. 'You heard what she said. He's come back!'

Lloyd sighed. 'Rubbish!' he said.

Their friend Ingrid said the same thing. Harvey telephoned her when they got back to the house, and she shouted with laughter.

'Come back? That's crazy! We saw him vanish.'

26

'But the Evolution Accelerator had a record of his DNA—'

'So?' Ingrid was scornful. 'It's been switched off for six months. Forget about him, Harvey. Now you're coming to live round here again, we're going to have *fun*. Mandy's cooked you a Welcome Back cake and Ian's discovered a fantastic new internet café.'

'Yes, but—'

'Stop butting. When are you getting here?'

Harvey gave up. 'In a couple of hours. We're setting out as soon as Mum and Dad get back with Dinah.'

'Great! I'll be there!' Ingrid said. 'And so will Ian and Mandy. SPLAT for ever!'

'SPLAT for ever!'

Harvey put the phone down and turned round. Lloyd was standing in the kitchen doorway, watching him.

'You see?' he said. 'Ingrid thinks it's rubbish too.'

'But we're still SPLAT,' Harvey muttered. 'The Society for the Protection of Our Lives Against Them. We ought to be ready—'

'There's nothing to be ready *for*!' Lloyd said.

3

Michael

They reached the new house an hour later than Harvey had predicted, because their parents hung around at the Research Centre talking to Claudia.

'*Such* a nice woman!' Mrs Hunter said when they came back. 'You'd never think she was a professor!'

'That's right,' Mr Hunter agreed. 'And she and Dinah get on like old friends.'

They went on talking about her most of the way to the new house, until Harvey was wriggling with impatience. He didn't care about Claudia Rowe. He wanted to arrive before Ingrid and the others got bored and went home.

He should have known better. Even though they were an hour late, Ingrid, Mandy, and Ian were sitting in a row on the front garden wall, chatting to the removal men.

'Here we are!' Ingrid shouted cheerfully. 'SPLAT support!'

'We've come to help you with the unpacking,' said Mandy.

Mrs Hunter jumped out of the car and gave them all a hug. 'It's lovely to see you! But you don't have to help.'

'Of course we do!' Ian said. 'It'll be great. Like a party. We'll come every day, until you're straight.'

They were as good as their promise. For three days, they all worked flat out. After three days, Mr Hunter started his new job and had to go off to California, but there was no let-up for the rest of them. They went on for another two days, until everything was unpacked.

And they'd all told so many jokes that Dinah felt weak from laughing.

'I don't think I've ever heard so many silly riddles in my whole life.'

'So?' Ingrid said. She was standing on Dinah's bed, balancing a book on her nose. 'What d'you want? *Solemn* riddles? *Sensible* jokes?'

Dinah grinned. 'No one tells sensible jokes. Not even a computer.'

She was just trying to think what a sensible joke would be like, when the phone rang, and Mrs Hunter called up the stairs.

'Dinah! It's for you!'

Clambering over three piles of books, Dinah ran downstairs and picked up the phone. 'Hello?'

'Hello!' said Claudia's voice. 'How's the new house? Got any good creepers growing in the garden?'

Dinah laughed. 'Haven't you got enough creeper?' Claudia had driven off from the Biogenetic

Research Centre with her boot crammed full of samples.

'Don't!' Claudia groaned. 'It's making my office into a jungle.'

'Is it any use?'

'Oh yes. That's why I'm phoning. I've made a breakthrough in my research, and I wondered if you'd like to come and take a look. How about tomorrow?'

'Tomorrow?' Dinah hesitated. 'I'd love to, but I don't know if I can come then. We're still unpacking—'

'Rubbish!' said her mother. She was standing right behind Dinah. 'It's that nice Professor Rowe, isn't it? If she's inviting you to visit her, you go. You've done your share of the unpacking.'

Dinah smiled over her shoulder. 'Thanks, Mum.' Then she spoke down the phone. 'Yes, please. I'd love to come tomorrow.'

'I don't know exactly where your house is, but it should only take you about twenty minutes on the bus,' Claudia said. 'Go to the main entrance and ask for my office. About eleven. Bring your brothers too, if they want to come.'

Dinah put the phone down and raced up the stairs.

'Lloyd! Harvey! I'm going to the university tomorrow, to see Claudia! Do you want to come?'

30

There was a wail and Ingrid came out of the bedroom pulling a face. 'You *can't* go to the university tomorrow! Don't be such a swot, Di. We want to go to the internet café.'

Dinah hesitated. It sounded fun, but she did want to go and see Claudia.

'Why can't you do both?' Ian said helpfully. He was coming upstairs with his arms full of coat hangers. 'You can go to the university and meet us for lunch at the café afterwards.'

'Great!' Ingrid beamed. 'I want to show you these new web sites I've found out about.'

There's more than one way of finding things out, Dinah thought, the next morning. She had just got off the bus, and she was walking down the slope, on to the university campus.

All round her, people were finding out, exploring ideas. Studying different kinds of knowledge in the different buildings. She read the names of the departments as she passed. English and American Studies. Engineering. Law. Social Sciences.

Beyond them all, at the far end of the campus, was the university library. Dinah's mind spun at the thought of all the knowledge in there, packed into books and magazines and disks.

She was so busy daydreaming that she stumbled

31

into the carved stone outside the next building and fell over. Rubbing her shins, she sat up and read the words on the stone. Artificial Intelligence Unit.

Well, it wasn't a very intelligent place to put a stone! Brushing the grass off her jeans, she scrambled up and looked round for the Biological Sciences building where Claudia worked.

It was opposite. A tall, greenish block with a front wall made entirely of glass. Claudia's room was right at the top and Dinah went up in the lift. That was glass too, and as she went up she stared out at the rest of the campus.

There was a man coming out of the Artificial Intelligence Unit. He was small and thin and he looked oddly out of place. His brown anorak didn't look like something a student or a lecturer would wear. Dinah wondered who he was.

The lift stopped at the top of the building. As the doors slid open, Dinah heard a boy's voice from the room across the corridor. He sounded angry and upset.

'He was horrible! He said, *Curiosity is the curse of the human brain!*'

'Oh come *on*, Michael!' That was Claudia. She sounded kind, but disbelieving. 'You must have misunderstood. No scientist would say that. Science is *about* curiosity.'

32

'He did say it!' The boy's voice was shrill and insistent.

'Well . . . maybe it was a joke.'

'It wasn't a joke!'

Dinah stood outside the door, not quite sure what to do. She didn't want to eavesdrop, but there didn't seem to be any way to avoid it.

On the other side of the door, Claudia made a soothing noise. 'He's under a lot of stress, you know. This Hyperbrain Conference he's planning is very big.'

'I know!' There was a defiant note in the boy's voice. 'He's told me all about it. He *always* tells me about his work. That's why it was so peculiar this morning. Don't you understand?'

He didn't wait for a reply. Flinging the door open, he raced out of the room, pushing Dinah to one side and jumping into the lift. Dinah had a brief glimpse of a round, freckled face with grubby glasses and uncombed hair. Then the lift doors closed and the boy slid out of sight.

Claudia came to the door and called after him. 'Michael! Wait!' But it was no use. She sighed, and beckoned Dinah into the room. 'I'm sorry. That wasn't a very nice welcome.'

'It doesn't matter,' Dinah said. 'But he did sound upset.'

Claudia sighed again and shut the door. 'I wish

33

he'd stayed to meet you. You're just the sort of friend he needs. He finds it hard to get on with most people, because he's so wrapped up in his father's research.'

'His father's a scientist?'

Claudia nodded. 'He's Tim Dexter.'

'The one who wrote that fantastic book about artificial intelligence?' Dinah's mouth dropped open.

'You *are* well-informed!' Claudia said. She smiled. 'Yes, that's him. He's a really nice guy, but he's up to his eyes in work at the moment, organizing a conference about artificial intelligence. I think Michael's feeling neglected.'

'Is it a big conference?'

Claudia nodded. '*Everyone* will be there. That's pretty frightening, because I'm giving the first paper.'

'But you're a biologist,' Dinah said. 'What's that got to do with computer intelligence?'

'Aha! That's what I want to tell you about. Artificial intelligence needs a phenomenal amount of memory, and I've cracked the information storage problem. Using molecular structures.'

'Using . . . what?'

'I'll show you.' Claudia looked pleased with herself. 'I've been working on it for years, but it was your creeper that helped me crack the problem.

The DNA structure is really intriguing. Come and look at what I've made.'

She led Dinah across to her desk and handed her a dull, heavy cylinder, about the size of a coffee jar.

'There you are. The world's first Molecular Storage Unit.'

Dinah turned it over in her hands. 'But . . . what's it made of? How does it work?'

'*That's* the interesting part. Take a look at these calculations . . . '

By the time she left Claudia, Dinah's head was buzzing with new ideas. She wouldn't have given Michael another thought, if she hadn't bumped into him again. Literally. He came charging out of the Artificial Intelligence Unit, and ran straight into her.

'Hey!' Dinah said crossly. 'Don't you ever walk? You ought to—'

Then she recognized him. And she remembered what Claudia had said. *You're just the sort of friend he needs.* She stopped glaring and grinned.

'Claudia said your father wrote that book— *Electronic Einstein.*'

Michael blinked and looked at her suspiciously. 'So?'

'So it's brilliant! I've read it twice.'

'It's not bad,' Michael said. 'But his new project's way ahead of that stuff. It's—' He stopped.

'Secret?' Dinah said.

'Oh no. It's just—' Michael shuffled his feet. 'Well . . . people usually get bored when I start talking about it.'

Dinah laughed. 'Not me. I think artificial intelligence is fascinating.'

'Really?'

'Really. I'd like to hear all about your father's research.'

Michael looked at her as if he couldn't believe his luck. His face blossomed into a smile. 'Well, if you're sure—'

That was the moment when Dinah remembered that she'd promised to meet the others for lunch. But she couldn't walk out on Michael. Not when she'd just got him to smile.

'Look,' she said quickly. 'I'm going to the internet café. Why don't you come too? Then we'll have lots of time to talk.'

'That would be great, but I'm not sure—'

'Can't we go and ask your father?'

Michael glanced back at the Artificial Intelligence Unit. For a second, Dinah thought he was going to say no. Then he grinned.

'OK. Want to come in and meet him?'

'Of course.'

There was a security lock on the door. Dinah thought they would have to buzz to get in, but Michael tapped the number straight on to the keypad. When he saw Dinah looking surprised, he grinned.

'Dad says I help him so much that I'm part of the department.'

He led the way in. The Unit wasn't very large. A couple of offices opened off each side of the square hallway, and there was another room at the back, opposite the front door. Tim Dexter's office was the first on the right. Michael knocked and pushed the door open.

'Dad?'

'Hi, Mike.' The man at the desk looked up. He had a young, freckled face, very like Michael's, and his denim jacket was covered with badges. He noticed Dinah and smiled at her. 'Are you a friend of Michael's?'

Dinah held out her hand. 'I'm Dinah Hunter. Claudia Rowe's working on some creeper I found.'

'Oh *yes*!' Tim Dexter jumped up. 'Claudia told me all about it. You've done the Hyperbrain a big favour!'

'There's really going to be an international Hyperbrain?' Dinah said.

She couldn't stop herself sounding excited, and Tim Dexter laughed.

'There certainly is. It'll take everyone years to agree, of course, but we're on the way. I wish I had time to tell you all about it.'

Dinah seized her chance. 'Michael's going to tell me. If he can come and have lunch in the internet café.'

'Great idea!' Tim Dexter fished in his pocket and pulled out some money. 'There you are, Mike. Have a good time.' He was still smiling when they left the room.

Dinah grinned at Michael. 'He's really nice, isn't he? You'd never think he was such a famous man.'

'He's great,' Michael said. 'He—'

He stopped as someone came in through the front door of the Unit. It was the man in the brown anorak that Dinah had seen before. He looked them up and down, with a strange, cold stare, and then knocked on the blue door opposite Tim Dexter's office.

'Who's that?' Dinah said, as he went inside. 'He doesn't look very nice.'

Michael's smile disappeared. 'He's OK,' he said gruffly. 'It's the other one who's horrible.'

'What other one?'

'The tall one.' Michael scowled at the blue door.

'He turned up a couple of days ago and started bossing everyone round. Tried to tell my dad that he shouldn't let children into the Unit.'

'But I thought your dad was in charge.'

'He is. And he'll sort it out after the conference. When he's not so busy.' Michael pushed the door open and stepped outside. 'Don't let's talk about that. I was going to tell you about the Hyperbrain, wasn't I?'

'Great!' Dinah forgot about the man behind the blue door and they talked about the Hyperbrain, all the way to the internet café.

4

The Internet Café

The others had been at the internet café for hours. Lots of people were eating and drinking but Lloyd and Harvey just stood behind Ian and Mandy and Ingrid as they wrote their messages.

Hey, Plum and Jelly, say hi to our friends, tapped in Ingrid.

'Plum and Jelly?' said Harvey.

'That's what they call themselves.' Ingrid leaned forward. 'And here's their answer.'

It didn't make sense to Lloyd. *Greetings from the Outdoor Centre. Tell them to try toenail clippings.*

'Try what?' he said.

Ingrid hooted with laughter.

'It's a silly game,' said Mandy. 'They choose something, and we have to guess how many times it appears on the Net.'

Harvey stared. 'Toenail clippings are on the Net?'

'Everything's on,' Ian said. 'But how many times?'

Lloyd hadn't got the faintest idea. 'Six?'

Ingrid grinned and shook her head, but she typed it in. The answer came back almost immediately.

:-D from Plum and Jelly.

'They're laughing at you,' Mandy said. 'I think you've got it totally wrong.'

'Got what wrong?' said a voice behind them.

It was Dinah. She was coming into the café with a boy Lloyd had never seen before. A pale, scruffy boy with glasses. He looked younger than Harvey and Ingrid. And much less fun. Lloyd felt like groaning.

'This is Michael,' Dinah said. 'His dad works at the university.'

Mandy smiled. 'Is he another biologist? Like Claudia Rowe?'

'He's Tim Dexter,' the boy said.

'So?' said Lloyd. 'Are we supposed to have heard of him?'

'He's famous,' Dinah said. She gave Lloyd a look that meant *Don't be mean.* 'He does computer research into artificial intelligence. He's setting up something called the Hyperbrain.'

'The Hyperbrain?' Ingrid gave a hoot of laughter. 'Sounds like science fiction.'

Harvey began strutting around stiffly. 'I. Am. The. Hyper. Brain. I. Will. Ex. Ter. Min. Ate. You.'

'Don't be an idiot!' Mandy said. She smiled at Michael again. 'Where's he building this Hyperbrain? At the university?'

41

Michael shook his head. 'It's not like that.' His voice was small and squeaky. 'It's going to be all over the world. Dad—'

Now he had started talking, he was speaking at top speed.

'—Dad's worked out a way of linking hundreds of computers, all over the world. And they'll really *think*—like a human brain! It'll be the biggest brain in the world, and—'

'Yuck!!' Ingrid pulled a face. 'A monster brain?' She started wobbling around. '*I am the Hyperbrain! I am the Hyperbrain!*'

'So people will be able to talk to it?' Lloyd said. 'And ask it what it thinks?'

Michael nodded.

'Weird!' said Ian. He reached over and pretended to type on the keyboard. '*What do you think about toenail clippings?* It's a pretty awkward way to have a conversation.'

'We won't be using keyboards,' Michael said scornfully. 'Or mice. Dad says they're "primitive interfaces". He's designing a completely new way to talk to the Hyperbrain. An advanced interface—'

Ingrid gave a last, enormous jelly-wobble and landed in Mandy's lap. 'It sounds great! When can we come and see it?'

Michael stared at her. 'See what?'

'The Hyperbrain. Can we come tomorrow?'

'You don't understand,' Michael said. 'It'll be years before it's ready.'

'You mean it doesn't exist?' Ingrid was outraged. 'So your dad hasn't really done *anything*?'

'Of course he has!' Michael went red in the face. 'He's done more for artificial intelligence than anyone in *history*! His Hyperbrain conference is going to be *huge*! There's even going to be a programme about it on *television*!'

'OK, OK.' Lloyd patted him on the shoulder. 'Don't blow a fuse.'

'You don't have to take any notice of Gerbil-Brain,' said Harvey.

'Gerbil-Brain?' shrieked Ingrid. 'What do you mean, Custard-Face?' She launched herself at Harvey and he dodged away between the tables.

'Oh no!' Mandy said. 'They'll get us thrown out!' She jumped up too, and ran after them.

Michael stared. He looked completely bewildered. Hadn't he ever heard of fun? Lloyd began to feel sorry for him.

'He's really lonely,' Dinah said. 'Can't we ask him round, Mum?'

She and her mother were in the garden, unpegging the washing. Mrs Hunter smiled at her round the side of a sheet.

43

'Of course we can. What about his parents? Should we ask them as well?'

'I think his dad's too busy at the moment. And his mum's in Australia, on a lecture tour.'

Mrs Hunter frowned. 'So who looks after him?'

'There's a person called Mrs Barnes. She's a housekeeper or something, but she doesn't sound much fun.'

'Poor little soul! Why don't you ask him round? We can have a barbecue and invite the others as well.'

'That's great!' Dinah beamed. 'Can it be next week? His father's got a big conference on Wednesday, and Michael can tell us all about it.'

Mrs Hunter smiled again. 'I don't see why not. You'll enjoy that—and the others can always talk about something else.'

'You never know,' Dinah said. 'They might even talk about the conference, if they watch it on television first.'

It looked as if she could be right. When she went back into the sitting room on Wednesday evening, to turn on the television, Lloyd and Harvey both trailed in after her.

'Are they going to show everything that happened at the conference?' Lloyd said.

Dinah shook her head. 'That would take hours. It's just highlights. The opening speeches and stuff like that.' She picked up the television magazine and flipped through. 'Oh bother, it's started already.'

She turned on, and they found themselves looking at a hall full of people.

'Bor*ing*!' Harvey said. 'Can't we watch the football instead?'

'Sssh!' Dinah said impatiently. 'Look, there's Claudia in the audience. I wonder why she looks so fed up? And there's—'

It was the man in the brown anorak. The man she had seen in the Artificial Intelligence Unit. But, before she could point him out to the others, the picture changed and she leaned forward excitedly. 'Look! That's Michael's dad up on the stage.'

Tim Dexter was standing at a lectern, making a speech.

' . . . never been a conference like this before . . . if we can agree to pool our computer resources . . . '

Harvey pulled a face. 'Sounds dull.'

'Of course it's not dull!' Dinah said impatiently. 'He's talking about the Hyperbrain. Listen!'

Harvey pulled another face, but Lloyd sat down and started watching.

'Lay off, Harvey. I want to hear what's going on.'

Tim Dexter seemed to be announcing some change of plan. ' . . . a slight alteration to our programme . . . We shall not now be hearing from Claudia Rowe about her development of Molecular Storage Units.'

'What?' Dinah said. 'But Claudia's spent *months* writing that speech! No wonder she looks annoyed. She—'

'Sssh!' said Lloyd. He was trying to work out what was going on. The people in the audience were all turning to look at each other, and there was a buzz of whispering.

'They're surprised too,' Harvey said. He sat down on the other side of Dinah.

Michael's father was still talking. ' . . . instead, we have a completely unexpected speaker, who has some exciting new developments in technology to tell us about. He—'

They couldn't hear the next words, because the screen suddenly went funny and the picture dissolved into chaos.

Lloyd grabbed the remote control and flicked through the other channels, until he got a picture again. He switched back to the conference and they saw Tim Dexter, beaming and holding out his hand.

'I'm very proud to introduce him. Here he is!'

They had a brief, blurred glimpse of a tall figure

46

walking on to the stage and then the picture disintegrated completely, into a pattern of tingling dots.

A moment later, letters spread themselves across the screen.

WE APOLOGIZE FOR THE LOSS OF SOUND AND PICTURES. THIS IS DUE TO CIRCUM-STANCES BEYOND OUR CONTROL.

'Oh, *brilliant*!' Harvey said. 'Why waste time talking about a Hyperbrain? They can't even invent televisions that don't break down.'

Dinah was still staring at the screen. Lloyd waved his hand in front of her face.

'Hey, square eyes, there's nothing on.'

'What?' She blinked and turned round. 'I was just thinking. It's pretty odd to change a conference speaker at the last moment. Especially at such an important conference. There were all sorts of people there—from universities and newspapers and all the media—everyone. And Claudia can't have been ill. I saw her.'

'So why didn't she give her lecture?' said Harvey.

'I don't know, but I bet she was furious. I'm going to see her again next week. I'll ask her what happened.'

'I wonder who they had instead of her,' said

Lloyd. 'He must be pretty important. It's a pity the television broke down before we saw him properly.'

5

A Shock for Dinah

There was nothing about the Hyperbrain Conference in the next day's newspaper, either. In fact, there was nothing all the week. When Dinah set off for her second visit to Claudia, she was looking forward to hearing what had happened. She jumped off the bus the moment it arrived at the university, and ran down the slope on to the campus.

She was running too fast for her own good. If she hadn't had very quick reactions, she would probably have landed up in hospital. A white van came roaring along the road at the bottom of the slope, so fast that she only just pulled herself out of the way in time.

'Crazy!' she muttered.

The van swung left, driving round to the back of the Artificial Intelligence Unit. For a second, Dinah glimpsed a green emblem painted on its side. She was peering after it, trying to make out what the emblem was, when her attention was distracted by a group of students coming through the front door of the Unit.

There was something bizarre about them.

Individually, they looked like ordinary students, in jeans and trainers and jumpers—but they were all wearing the same kind of jeans and trainers, and their jumpers were exactly the same shape. It was as if they were wearing a uniform.

They went past Dinah without even looking at her, and she was still glancing back at them when she reached the Biological Sciences building. As she went up in the lift, she could see them marching through the campus, side by side, without speaking to each other.

Then the lift reached the top, and she forgot all about them. The thought of finding out about the conference was much more interesting. Running out of the lift, she knocked on the door of Claudia's office.

There was no answer.

Dinah frowned and looked at her watch. She wasn't early. And Claudia had sounded really keen for them to meet again. *Come and hear all about the conference*, she'd said. *I'll enjoy telling you.* She couldn't just have forgotten. Not even if she was upset about having her speech dropped from the conference programme.

Dinah waited two or three minutes and knocked again, more loudly. This time, footsteps came across the room. The door opened and Claudia looked out at her.

'Hello!' Dinah smiled brightly. 'How was the conference? I couldn't watch——'

Her voice died away. Claudia wasn't smiling back. She was looking at her as if she were a stranger.

'You did . . . remember I was coming?' Dinah said nervously.

'Of course I remembered.' Claudia's voice was cold and distant. 'But I'm busy.' She began to turn away.

Dinah couldn't believe her ears. 'But you asked me to come! You said you'd tell me about the conference.'

Claudia turned back. She was wearing an odd little badge on her blouse and it caught the light for a moment, making Dinah blink. 'What happened at the conference is none of your business,' she said. 'It is confidential scientific information.'

Dinah stared. 'But I thought scientists shared their knowledge. I thought that was the point of conferences.'

'Knowledge is too precious to waste on ordinary people,' Claudia said stiffly.

It didn't make sense. How could she be saying things like that? Dinah was bewildered. 'I don't want you to tell me anything secret. But I can't help being curious——'

51

She didn't get any further. The moment she said *curious*, Claudia's eyes glazed over. 'Curiosity is the curse of the human brain,' she said.

'What?' Dinah couldn't believe her ears. 'But that's what Michael's father said. And you told Michael no scientist would say it!'

Claudia didn't answer. She stood perfectly still, staring at Dinah. Waiting for her to go away.

It was like a nightmare. Dinah saw herself reflected in Claudia's dull, glassy eyes. Two tiny Dinahs. Puzzled and miserable. She edged away, and the little green badge on Claudia's blouse caught her reflection as well, like a third eye.

Three tiny, miserable Dinahs.

For a moment, the two of them stood facing each other, without a word. Then the phone started to ring inside Claudia's office. She turned away to answer it and Dinah hurried into the lift. The noise of the telephone echoed down the stairwell, repeating like the word that hammered in her brain: *Why? . . . Why? Why? . . . Why?*

Before the lift reached the ground, the ringing had stopped. As she pushed the front door open, Dinah heard someone calling.

'Dinah!'

It was Claudia. Glancing over her shoulder, Dinah saw her face staring down from the top floor.

'Dinah! Come back!' she shouted.

For a second, Dinah thought, *It's all right! It was all a mistake.*

Then she saw Claudia's face. It still wasn't smiling. She was leaning over the banisters and peering down with the same glazed expression as before. And when she called again, there was an odd, shrill note in her voice.

'Dinah! Wait!'

I can't, Dinah thought. *I can't.*

She ran outside and dodged away round the side of the building. Looking back nervously over her shoulder, she saw the empty lift swoop up to the top floor again. Claudia stepped into it and reached out to press a button. Still looking behind her, Dinah bumped hard into someone coming the other way.

It was Michael.

'You're getting like me,' he said cheerfully. Then he saw her face. 'What's up?'

'I—' Dinah took a deep breath. 'I've just been to see Claudia. And she was horrible.'

'*Claudia?*'

Dinah nodded miserably. 'She wasn't like herself. She—'

Claudia's voice called again, from just round the corner.

'Dinah! Where are you?'

It was even shriller than before. Dinah grabbed Michael's arm.

'I can't talk to her!' she hissed. 'I know it's silly, but . . . I can't. Where can I hide?'

Michael didn't waste time arguing. 'Come into the AIU,' he whispered. Running down the path, he punched in the security code and pushed the door open. 'We can go to Dad's office.'

But they had hardly stepped inside the building when Tim Dexter appeared. He looked much the same as he had the last time Dinah visited the Unit—the same untidy clothes, covered in badges—but this time he was obviously not pleased to see her.

'What are you doing here?' he said coldly.

Michael looked startled. 'We've just come in to see you. I was going to show Dinah—'

'This isn't a place for visitors.'

'But, Dad—'

'I'll see you at home, Michael. When I've finished work.'

Michael's mouth dropped open. Dinah could see that he was completely amazed.

'It's OK,' she said quickly. 'We can go somewhere else. Come on, Michael.'

Tim Dexter looked as if he meant to stand watching them until they left. But the phone began to ring in his office. He gave them a last glance

54

and said briskly, 'Off you go.' Then he turned and went back inside.

Miserably, Dinah pushed the front door open. 'Why is everyone suddenly being horrible?' she said.

Michael fired up. 'Dad's not horrible!'

'Oh, I'm sorry!' Dinah suddenly realized how her words must have sounded. 'I didn't mean—'

But Michael wouldn't let her finish. 'Dad's *not* horrible,' he said again. 'It's *him*. He's the one who's done it!' He glared at the blue door opposite his father's office as he followed Dinah out of the building.

Dinah looked back at it—and saw that there was a notice on it. She was sure it hadn't been there last time.

Controller, it said.

She frowned. 'If your dad's in charge—what's that?'

Michael's lips pinched together. 'It happened after the conference. *He* took over.' He nodded towards the door.

'He? You mean the man in the brown anorak?'

'Of course not,' Michael said scornfully. 'Brown Anorak just runs the errands. It's the other one who's taken over.'

A small, cold shiver ran down Dinah's back. A lot of odd things had happened that day. She found herself remembering the warm feel of the Evolution

Accelerator under her fingers. She'd never mentioned it to the others, in case they laughed at her, but suddenly it seemed horribly threatening.

She took a deep breath. 'This other man. Is he——?'

But she didn't get any further. Michael suddenly grabbed at her sleeve.

'Look out! There's Claudia!'

Back at the Hunters' house, Lloyd was telephoning Ian.

Or, rather, he was *trying* to telephone Ian. The first three times he dialled, nothing happened at all. The fourth time, he got through, but the line was so bad that he could hardly make out a word.

'Is that you, Ian?'

'Hzzz there? I czzzz harzzz oosssssh.'

'Ian! It's Lloyd!'

'Czzzzzzz hooosssh wozzzzoooza.'

'Can you hear me?'

Mrs Hunter put her head over the banisters and called down to him.

'Is that wretched phone still bad? I tried to phone Dinah's friend earlier on. The boy at the university. I was trying to tell him what time to come for the barbecue, but I don't suppose he understood a word.'

'I'm not surprised.' Lloyd looked at the phone in disgust. It was making noises like a storm at sea now. 'I can't even tell if this *is* Ian.' He gave up and put it down.

'It's a nuisance,' Mrs Hunter said. 'You'll just have to go round to see Ian and Mandy and Ingrid. Tell them to be here at half-past six.'

Lloyd pulled a face, but he could see that she was right. 'Come on, Harvey. We'll go to Ian's first. Maybe we can phone the others from there.'

'Tell them not to bring anything,' Mrs Hunter said. 'This is a thank you barbecue, because they've helped us so much. And tell Ingrid I'll make her some really hot chilli sauce.'

Harvey groaned. 'Death By Chilli?'

'Is that what she calls it?' Mrs Hunter laughed. 'I don't know how she can eat the stuff, but she adores it, doesn't she? I must go and find the recipe.'

She rattled downstairs and disappeared into the kitchen. Lloyd picked up the phone for one last attempt at getting through to Ian. This time there wasn't even a dialling tone. Only a noise like aliens twittering to each other. He slammed it down and opened the front door.

'Come on then, Harvey. Let's spread the news the Stone Age way. I'll race you to Ian's.'

6

The Green Hand

'Claudia's coming!' Michael said again.

She must have been to the bus stop, because she was coming back down the slope again. Dinah looked round wildly.

'What am I going to do?'

'Hide round at the back of the Unit.' Michael pointed. 'I'll come and tell you when she's gone.'

Dinah ran down the side of the AIU building and crouched behind a clump of bushes. From there, she could see Michael's back. And although she couldn't see Claudia, she could hear her voice clearly.

'Michael!' Claudia was calling. 'Have you seen Dinah?'

'Dinah?' Michael's voice was vague. Dinah could tell that he was playing for time. 'Do you mean—'

'I mean Dinah Hunter,' Claudia said impatiently. 'I must find Dinah Hunter.'

'Oh, *Dinah*.' Michael hesitated. 'No, I haven't really—'

Peering out of the bushes, Dinah saw him shifting from foot to foot. *Claudia's never going to believe him*, she thought. *She's going to guess—*

But it didn't happen, because, just at that moment Tim Dexter came hurrying out of the AIU.

'Michael!' he said briskly. 'Where's that friend of yours? The one you brought in just now?'

Dinah felt herself grow icy-cold. Was he looking for her as well? What was going on?

Whatever it was, it made Michael pull himself together. 'You mean Dinah? She's on her way home,' he said firmly. 'She was really upset about something.'

There was a funny little noise from Claudia, but she didn't say anything. Peering out, Dinah saw her march off to the Biological Sciences building and into the lift.

Tim Dexter sighed with impatience. 'Bring that girl to see me as soon as you can,' he said. Then he turned and went back to his office as well.

Michael walked slowly down the side of the AIU building, looking puzzled and unhappy.

'That was *weird*,' he whispered as he reached Dinah. 'Why does everyone want to talk to you all of a sudden?'

Dinah shrugged. 'Maybe it's something to do with the creeper. And those Molecular Storage things.'

'I suppose so,' Michael said doubtfully.

'Perhaps I'll phone Claudia when I get home. Before the barbecue.'

59

'Oh . . . the barbecue.' Michael's face cleared, as though he'd suddenly remembered something. 'That's why I came to look for you in the first place. What time shall I come?'

'Didn't Mum tell you? I thought she was going to phone this afternoon.'

Michael nodded. 'I think she did. Someone phoned anyway, but the line was so bad I couldn't understand a word.'

'Never mind. You can come back with me. It won't matter if we're early. We can go now, if the coast is clear.'

'I'll go and see.' Cautiously, Michael walked back to the corner of the building and peered round. Glancing back at Dinah, he started to beckon her— and then stopped, suddenly.

'What's the matter?' Dinah hissed. 'Is Claudia coming back?'

Michael shook his head. 'Nothing like that,' he muttered. 'It's just—' He was staring up the campus towards the huge university library. 'There's something peculiar happening. Come and look.'

By five o'clock, Lloyd and Harvey were setting up the barbecue. They'd just assembled it when their mother came out of the kitchen.

'My barbecue book wasn't in that box, was it?'

Lloyd picked the box up and shook it. Nothing fell out except an old paper cup.

Mrs Hunter frowned. 'I can't find my chilli sauce recipe.'

'So?' Lloyd said. 'Make something else.'

'But I promised Ingrid. And she really loves it. I can't find a recipe anywhere.'

'No problem,' Lloyd said. 'There's bound to be a barbecue book in that little library round the corner. Harvey can go down and find a recipe there.'

'Me?' Harvey looked indignant. 'Why can't you go?'

'I've got to light the barbecue, and Mum's making the salads. It has to be you.'

'But I don't know where—'

'Don't be so useless. It's the little building on the corner of Orchard Street.'

'It'll be shut,' Harvey said obstinately.

Mrs Hunter grinned. 'No it won't. It's open every afternoon until seven o'clock. I looked the other day. Go on, Harvey, there's a dear.'

Harvey went off, grumbling under his breath, and Mrs Hunter hurried back into the kitchen. *Thank goodness for that*, Lloyd thought. Now he could concentrate on lighting the barbecue without Harvey twittering round and telling him he was doing it all wrong.

61

He dragged the sack of charcoal out of the garage and filled the barbecue. Then he spent ten minutes hunting for the firelighters.

He'd only just found them when Harvey arrived back. He was red-faced and indignant.

'I told you! I said it would be shut! All that way for nothing!'

Lloyd frowned. 'But Mum said it was open every afternoon.'

'Not any more.' Harvey collapsed on to one of the patio chairs. 'It looks as if it's shut for good.'

'What are you talking about?' Lloyd forgot the barbecue and sat down too. 'Libraries don't just *shut*.'

'That one has. There's a big sign stuck on the front door. *Closed until further notice, owing to cuts.*'

'But there would be posters,' Lloyd said scornfully. 'People get up petitions about things like that. They make a terrible fuss.'

'It's shut,' Harvey said. 'There are men taking the books away in vans.'

Lloyd shook his head. 'That's very odd.'

'What's odd?' said a voice.

Lloyd looked round. Dinah and Michael were coming through the back door, and Dinah had caught his last few words.

She's going to be furious, Lloyd thought. Dinah read more library books than all of them put together.

Wherever they'd lived before, she'd always visited the library at least once a week. Now she'd have to go right into town. She was going to *explode* when she heard the news.

'What's odd?' she said again, rather sharply.

'You're not going to like it,' said Harvey.

'The library's closed down.' Lloyd held his breath, waiting for the explosion—but it didn't come. Instead, Dinah turned pale. She looked over her shoulder at Michael.

'Did you hear that?'

Michael nodded. His face was strange as well. 'What do you mean—closed?' he said.

'Shut,' Harvey said. 'Finished. They're taking the books away in vans.'

'White vans?' Michael said slowly. 'With a green hand painted on the side?'

Harvey looked startled. 'That's right. How did you know?'

Dinah sat down at the table. Her face was very pale now. 'It's happening at the university library as well. There's a big sign on the front door: *Closed until further notice, owing to maintenance.* And the car park at the back is full of Green Hand vans taking the books away.'

Lloyd shrugged. 'So? Maybe the Green Hand's a firm of bookbinders. Perhaps they're repairing all the old books round here.'

Michael shook his head. 'They weren't old books. It was all the new, expensive books they were loading up.'

'And there are other things, too,' Dinah said. She had gone very quiet, the way she did when she was really worried about something.

'Like?' Lloyd said.

Michael opened his mouth to answer, but Dinah shook her head. 'It's too serious to chat about,' she said. 'I think we ought to wait till the others come. And have a proper SPLAT meeting about it.'

'OK,' Lloyd said.

But he couldn't see why she was making such a fuss.

Nor could the others, at first.

'Perhaps it's just a coincidence about the vans,' Mandy said. 'They may not be the same at all. There are lots of white vans around.'

'With green hands on them?' said Dinah.

Ian was looking down at his own hand, wriggling the fingers around. 'Maybe they weren't the *same* Green Hands.'

Michael took a piece of paper out of his pocket. 'The ones at the university were like this.'

He began to sketch a shape in tiny, neat lines.

A square palm with long, clutching fingers like claws. Harvey watched him and nodded.

'The ones down the road were like that as well.'

Mandy shuddered. 'It looks horrible. Greedy. As if it wants to snatch everything away.'

'Oh, don't exaggerate!' said Ingrid. 'It's not snatching *everything*. Only books.'

Dinah was staring down at the little drawing as well, and her eyes were wide. 'I'm not sure it *is* only books,' she said softly. 'I've seen that hand somewhere else.'

Michael glanced up. He looked surprised. 'You have?'

Dinah nodded. 'I've just realized. Claudia had it too. On a badge.' There was an odd note in her voice. Almost scared.

'So?' Lloyd said. 'I thought you liked Claudia.'

'I did. But she was different today. Horrible.'

'And she had a Green Hand badge?' Ian said, trying to make sense of it all.

Dinah nodded. 'I didn't realize when I saw the vans, because the hand on them is so big. But seeing it little—the way Michael's drawn it—it was just the same!'

Slowly Michael picked up the pen again. He drew a small circle round the hand, to make it look like a badge. Then he gazed at it.

'My dad wears one, too,' he said, at last. 'His jacket's covered in badges, so I didn't notice it much, but I'm sure he's got one.'

Dinah leaned forward. 'Where did it come from?'

'From the Hyperbrain Conference. I think.'

Lloyd decided it was time he took charge. He sat down next to Dinah and rapped on the table. 'OK. This is a proper SPLAT meeting. Who's going to take notes?'

'I will.'

Mandy reached for Michael's piece of paper and drew a line under the picture of the Green Hand badge. Then she started to make a list of the things they'd said.

1. *Libraries are closing and Green Hand vans are taking the books away.*
2. *Michael's father came back from the Hyperbrain Conference with a Green Hand badge.*
3. *Claudia has a Green Hand badge.*

'And Claudia was at the Conference,' Michael said.

Lloyd looked down at the list. 'So it all started there?'

'Not exactly.' Michael frowned, gathering his thoughts. 'Dad started being strange before that. When those men came.' He glanced at Dinah. 'You

66

know—Brown Anorak and the other one. That was when Dad started to say peculiar things.'

'Like this?' Dinah said. She took the pen from Mandy and added another line to the list.

4. *Curiosity is the curse of the human brain.*

Michael looked at her in amazement. 'How did you know about that?'

'I overheard you telling Claudia. She said you must have misunderstood, didn't she? But today *she said it too*!'

She looked round at the others, and Lloyd could see that there was something else on her mind.

'Go on,' he said. 'Spit it out.'

Dinah looked down at her hands. 'Michael's dad and Claudia have both gone strange. And they're both saying the same thing. *Curiosity is the curse of the human brain.* It's as if—' She lifted her head and stared at Lloyd, challenging him. '—as if they've been hypnotized.'

7

Crazyspace

Michael didn't understand, but the others did. Dinah saw their faces change, and Lloyd erupted, just as she knew he would.

'You're as bad as Harvey! He kept going on about the Headmaster when we were at the Research Centre. That's all nonsense! You saw him disappear into the Evolution Accelerator.'

'Yes,' Dinah said. 'But it recorded his DNA, didn't it? That's all it needs, you know, to . . . ' She hesitated and then forced herself to say it. ' . . . to make a clone.'

'A *clone*?' Michael's mouth dropped open. 'What are you talking about? And who's the Headmaster?'

'He used to be at our school,' Lloyd said grimly. 'He hypnotizes people.'

'And he wants to take over everything.' Dinah ran her finger lightly over the Green Hand drawing. 'To grab it, like this, and make it totally efficient.'

'So?' Michael was looking more and more bewildered. 'What's wrong with efficiency? We could do with a bit more of it in our house, I can tell you.'

He grinned, but no one grinned back. Mandy shook her head.

'You don't understand. He doesn't just make things run smoothly. He makes people do exactly what *he* wants. And he doesn't care about feelings or differences between people. He'd like the whole world to be a sort of machine.'

Ingrid frowned. 'But if this Controller person is him—why is he bothering with people at a university? What's he going to take over? The rugby team?'

'It's the other teams he needs to hypnotize,' Harvey said. He gazed into Ingrid's eyes. '*You are feeling too sleepy to tackle anyone. Funny how you keep falling over . . .* '

Ingrid grinned and slumped sideways. This time it was Michael who didn't smile.

'There's other things at the university, besides the rugby team,' he said. His fingers tightened round the drawing of the Green Hand, screwing it into a little, crumpled ball.

'Like what?' said Lloyd.

Michael swallowed. 'Like something very powerful. Powerful enough to deal with all the knowledge in the world.'

Dinah felt sick. 'The Hyperbrain.'

'That's right.' Michael nodded. 'If he's taken

that over, he can control all the major computers in the world.'

'But the Hyperbrain doesn't exist!' Ingrid said indignantly. 'You told us it wouldn't happen for *years*!'

'I know,' Michael said. He looked up, and his face was very pale. 'But when Dad came back from the conference he said it was ready to start. Because everyone had suddenly agreed, without any arguments at all. As if—'

'As if they'd been hypnotized,' said Mandy softly.

There was a long, unhappy silence.

Then Lloyd said, 'So you think the Headmaster's controlling all the knowledge in the world?'

Dinah nodded. 'And he's making sure no one else can get any.' She picked up the crumpled drawing of the Green Hand and smoothed it out. 'Don't you see? Books are already disappearing from libraries. And people are being told not to ask questions. Is that just round here, or is it everywhere? We've got to find out.'

'That'll be really easy!' Lloyd said sarcastically. 'Let's put an ad in the papers, shall we? *Please tell us if your library's closing. Let us know if your parents are hypnotized.* Get real, Di! We can't investigate all over the country.'

'Yes, we can,' Dinah said. 'We can use the internet.'

70

*　*　*

She knew exactly what she wanted to do. But they couldn't start until the next morning, when the internet café opened. And the next morning was a long time coming.

All night, she had nightmares. She dreamt she was back in the Biogenetic Research Centre, standing beside the Evolution Accelerator. In front of her, on the bench, was a mobile phone.

. . . on my way to the lab with Professor Rowe. From the University of Wessex.

Intelligence has all the power. It takes over everything! We can watch it all on the video.

The words resounded with meaning, as if they were the first words she'd ever heard. As if they were telling her crucial things about the world.

Intelligence has all the power . . .

In her dream, she reached out for the mobile phone—but the hand that reached out wasn't her own. It was pale and square, with long fingers, curved to grab . . .

She woke up with a scream, and found herself sitting bolt upright in bed.

'Dinah? Are you all right?' Mrs Hunter came running along the landing in her nightdress. 'What's the matter?'

'I—' Dinah caught her breath and rubbed a hand across her eyes. 'I had a bad dream. That's all.'

Mrs Hunter put an arm round her shoulders and hugged her. 'Is there something wrong?'

'I—' Dinah wanted to pour the whole thing out, but she knew what would happen. Mum wouldn't believe her. Or, if she did, she would tell her to be careful. And forbid her to investigate.

Dinah swallowed and managed rather a shaky smile. 'I'm fine. Just a bit . . . unsettled.'

Mrs Hunter gave her another hug. 'Never mind. All the moving's over now. Dad's got to travel about, because of his job, but we'll stay here, where your friends are.'

'That's great,' Dinah said. And she meant it. If she was right about the Green Hand badges, she was going to need SPLAT more than ever.

Mrs Hunter smiled. 'Have you got any plans for tomorrow?'

'We're meeting at the internet café. At half-past nine.'

'Better get some sleep then, or you'll be snoring over the computers.'

Dinah laughed and lay down, and her mother tucked the duvet round her.

But she couldn't sleep. She wanted to be doing something.

* * *

It was harder than she expected. When she arrived at the internet café next morning, with Lloyd and Harvey, Mandy and Ingrid were huddled over one of the computers. They were muttering unhappily.

'What's the matter?' Dinah said. 'Something wrong with the computer?'

Mandy shook her head. 'The computer's fine. It's the phone lines that are dodgy. We're having real trouble getting on the internet.'

'I'll try again,' Ingrid said doggedly. 'Hang on.'

She had to make three more attempts before they got a connection. When they did, she didn't waste any time.

'I'd better get chatting before we lose it again.'

How does the Green Hand grab you? she typed.

Answers began to appear immediately.

It came and grabbed us yesterday.

They took our library books away! — Plum and Jelly

Us too! It's a badge on the cadge, man! :-(— Griddlebone

That mangy mitt has sticky fingers! — Workaholic

'You see?' Dinah said. 'I knew it! It's going on everywhere! See if you can find out where they are!'

Ingrid's fingers reached for the keyboard again, but she didn't have time to type even a letter. Suddenly, the screen blacked out. There was a

73

confused flutter of lights and then a single message spread itself across the screen:

ACCESS TO SERVER SUSPENDED
CURIOSITY IS THE CURSE OF THE HUMAN
BRAIN

Ingrid groaned. 'Is it the phone line again?'
'I don't think so.' Lloyd looked round the café. 'Everyone else has lost it too.'

He was right. At all the computer tables, people were muttering angrily. And Dinah could see the same square letters spreading across every screen.

ACCESS TO SERVER SUSPENDED
CURIOSITY IS THE CURSE OF THE HUMAN
BRAIN

The only person still typing was a girl on the far side of the room. They'd never spoken to her, but she always seemed to be in the internet café, hunched over the same machine.

The man at the next table got up to see what she was doing. He came back looking disgusted.

'She's just on that kids' thing,' he said to the woman next to him. 'Crazyspace, or whatever it's called.'

'Typical.' Crossly, the woman picked up her briefcase. 'We can't do our work—but kids can

74

chat as much as they like.' She stamped out and most of the other adults followed.

Kids can chat as much as they like . . .

The words echoed in Dinah's head. Maybe they weren't finished after all. She got up and walked across to the girl.

'Hi. I'm Dinah.'

'I'm Kate.' The girl looked up and blinked as she saw the café emptying. 'What's up?'

'The server's packed up.' Dinah waved a hand at the blank screens. 'How come you're still on line?'

'I'm not on the internet,' Kate said. 'This is a separate network for kids to chat. Supposed to be *safer* than surfing the Net.' She pulled a funny face, and laughed.

Dinah didn't laugh back. She leaned forward, eagerly. 'So you can still chat? To people all over the place?'

'Only children.'

'Children will do fine.' Dinah pulled up a chair and sat down. 'Can you show us how to get in?'

Within ten minutes, Dinah had explained what was going on, and they were all huddled round Kate's screen. She obviously thought they were playing some kind of game, but she was quite happy to show them how to get into Crazyspace.

75

'You've got to do a bit of Crazyspeak, to show you belong.' Her fingers moved over the keys like lightning. She was twice as fast as Ingrid.

Seen a badge with a seasick mitt?

What did it grab? Was your library hit?

Mandy frowned. 'But that looks like nonsense.'

'Great!' said Ingrid. 'I bet that's why no one's closed the network down. They think it's just kids talking rubbish. Give this a go, Kate—'

Go on and tell us your place and the trouble it's in.

Is it hard to ask questions? Are the books getting thin?

The words went in almost as fast as she said them, and Ingrid reached over and added her signature—*Werewolf.*

Straight away, the first answer came flooding on to the screen:

Books and phones—we've lost them both.

GHB plague has hit Arbroath—Smoky.

Ian frowned. 'GHB?'

'Green Hand Badge, pea-brain.' Lloyd leaned closer. 'Look, here's another one.'

Badges, badges everywhere!

Get those green things out of our hair!

You should hear us moan and grouse.

We've got HUNDREDS in our house!

'Hundreds?' Ian frowned. 'What sort of house is it? The House of Commons?'

Harvey and Lloyd started laughing, but Ingrid

was peering at the screen and reading the rest of the message.

'No, look. It's *them*.'

'Them?' Dinah said.

'Plum and Jelly. They live in the country. In some sort of outdoor centre near Manchester.' Ingrid pointed at the last lines of the message.

(*Thought we'd lost you when the internet crashed. Fancy you knowing about Crazyspace too! You're a network queen, Werewolf! — Plum and Jelly.*)

Mandy was still looking puzzled. 'It's nice they've turned up again, but they're not making sense. Why would there be hundreds of badges in an outdoor centre?'

There was no time to work it out. The messages kept on pouring in, as if they'd unblocked a river.

No more smileys from Bettws y Coed.

Our borrowing has been destroyed.

Dinah began writing down the place names as fast as she could.

Cheltenham.

Cardiff.

Peterborough.

Arran.

Newcastle.

Truro.

There were still problems with the phone line, but the picture they were getting was clear, even

77

though messages kept being cut off in the middle. All over the country, there were libraries closing. And all over the country people had noticed Green Hand badges.

'It's terrible!' Kate said. She looked round at them all. 'What's going on?'

'That's what we're trying to find out,' Dinah said.

'But it's so complicated!' wailed Ingrid. 'You'd need a Hyperbrain to keep track of it.'

'There *is* a Hyperbrain keeping track of it,' Lloyd said. 'That's the point, you thicko.'

For the first time that day, Dinah thought about the Hyperbrain—and she remembered Michael. She put down her pen and looked round the café.

'Where's Michael? He said he'd be here at half-past nine, like the rest of us. It's almost eleven now.'

Lloyd shrugged. 'Must have got delayed. Maybe he forgot.'

'He wouldn't forget. He's very precise.' Dinah frowned. 'Go on writing the places down, Mandy. I'm going to phone him.'

There was a phone in the corner of the café and she spent ten minutes trying to get through, but it was no use. All she could hear was a jumbled buzzing noise. Finally, the telephone ate her money and refused to give it back.

78

She turned to go back to the table—and there was Michael. He was just walking into the café, and he looked dreadful. His face was pale and his eyes were red, as though he hadn't slept all night.

He spotted Dinah, and threw himself across the café towards her. 'Thank goodness you're still here!'

Dinah grabbed his shoulders and led him over to the others. 'Whatever is the matter?'

'It's my dad!'

'What do you mean? What's happened?'

Michael sat down suddenly in the nearest chair, as if his legs wouldn't hold him up.

'I can't find him anywhere. He's vanished!'

8

Your Wildest Dreams

So it's not just books, Lloyd thought. *The Green Hand's grabbing people now!*

He sat down next to Michael. 'What do you mean he's vanished?'

Michael looked up, and his face was desperate. 'He didn't come home yesterday. I waited up till midnight, but there wasn't a message. And there wasn't one this morning, either.'

'The phones have been weird,' Ingrid said doubtfully. 'Maybe he tried and he couldn't get through.'

Michael shook his head. 'It's not that simple. Mrs Barnes says he's gone to Brazil. But he would never go off like that, without telling me.'

'So what makes her think he's there?' said Dinah.

'The Controller told her he was!'

'The Controller?' Harvey said. 'You mean—?'

Michael nodded. 'Him. I think he's kidnapped Dad. I think he's got him hidden away somewhere.'

'But why?' Mandy said.

'I don't know. But I've got to find out.' Michael glanced round the internet café to make sure no one else was listening. Then he leaned forward and whispered. 'I'm going into the AIU tonight. To search for clues.'

He looked very small, and his voice was even squeakier than ever. Lloyd thought the whole idea sounded ridiculous.

But Dinah obviously didn't. 'I'll come with you,' she said.

It took Lloyd's breath away. 'But—'

'Someone's got to help him,' Dinah said fiercely. 'And I'm the best person, because I'll be able to help him search the Hyperbrain. If there are any clues, they're probably there.'

'But you can't go!' Harvey said. 'It's too dangerous, Di. You might meet the Headmaster—and he hates you.'

'Does he?' Dinah said. She grinned suddenly, and the others blinked at her.

'Of course he does,' Harvey said.

Dinah went on grinning. 'If this man in the AIU is made from the Headmaster's DNA, he'll be exactly like the Headmaster—but he won't have the Headmaster's memory. DNA only carries things you can inherit.'

'So?' Ingrid said.

'So he may have learnt things like language and science—there was a concentrated learning system at the Research Centre—but he can't have

81

learnt about me. Even if he does see me—*he won't recognize me!*'

Lloyd tried to imagine the Headmaster coming face to face with Dinah, staring at her with those terrible sea-green eyes—and then walking past without taking any notice. It didn't seem possible.

Dinah was happy about it, though. She was already going on with her plans. 'Has anybody got any change? I'll have a go at phoning Mum, to tell her I'm spending the night at Michael's.'

Mandy produced a couple of coins and Dinah went back to the phone. Lloyd and Harvey looked at each other.

'We can't let her go,' Harvey muttered.

Lloyd shrugged. 'We won't be able to stop her, if she's made up her mind. And I suppose she's right. Even if it is the Headmaster, he can't possibly remember her.'

Dinah was already on her way back from the phone box, looking annoyed.

'The phones are terrible! I thought I'd really got through this time. Then the line started crackling and we were cut off. It's no use going home, because Mum's going shopping at half-past four. You'll have to tell her, Lloyd.'

'Thanks.' Lloyd pulled a face. 'What am I supposed to say? *Hello, Mum. Dinah hasn't come home*

82

because she's going to break into the Artificial Intelligence unit tonight.'

'You'll think of something,' Dinah said. 'Come on, Michael.'

Harvey caught at her sleeve. 'Be careful.'

'Of course I will,' Dinah said. 'Don't worry. I don't want to see the Headmaster any more than you do. But I've got to go.'

She began heading out of the café, but Michael hesitated. When she reached the door, she looked back at him.

'What's the matter? Aren't you coming?'

'I just thought . . . ' he wavered. 'Are you sure you want to do this? What about Claudia?'

'I can dodge her,' Dinah said. 'Come *on*.'

She went outside and Michael started across the café after her.

'Hang on a minute,' Lloyd called. 'What did Dinah mean? Why does she have to dodge Claudia?'

'Claudia was looking for her,' Michael said. He reached the door himself and pushed it open. 'So was my dad. It was weird, really. They both got phone calls, and then—oh, sorry. There's a bus.'

Through the window, Lloyd saw Dinah beckoning, and pointing at the bus. Before any of them could stop her, she and Michael had jumped on the bus and gone.

Lloyd and Harvey looked at each other.

'We shouldn't have let her go,' Harvey said miserably.

As they went home, Harvey was still fretting.

'I hope Mum's furious,' he kept muttering. 'I hope she goes straight off to the university to fetch Dinah back. I hope—'

'Shut up!' muttered Lloyd. He wasn't looking forward to telling his mother that Dinah was away for the night.

But it turned out to be much easier than he expected.

'Look, Mum,' he began, when she came back from the shops, 'Dinah's gone off to stay the night at the university—'

And, before he could get any further, Mrs Hunter beamed. 'So *that's* what Claudia wanted!'

'I . . . I'm sorry?' Lloyd was confused.

'I couldn't make sense of her telephone call,' Mrs Hunter said. 'She phoned up at lunchtime, but the line was terrible. I thought she was saying *I want to find Dinah today*. But it must have been *I want to have Dinah to stay*.'

Lloyd and Harvey glanced at each other. 'I . . . er . . . yes,' Lloyd said. He didn't like the sound of that telephone call, but at least it saved a lot of awkward explaining.

And Mrs Hunter was delighted. 'I'm so glad Dinah's in touch with Claudia again. It sounded as if there was something wrong last time, but it's obviously been sorted out.'

From the corner of his eye, Lloyd saw Harvey get ready to speak. The idiot! He wasn't going to tell Mrs Hunter she'd made a mistake, was he? That would start all sorts of trouble.

Lloyd kicked out at Harvey's ankle. He only meant it as a warning, but he hit it rather harder than he intended. Harvey ran off, with a snort of rage, and Mrs Hunter looked up.

'What's the matter with him?'

'Haven't got a clue,' Lloyd said innocently.

He heard Harvey go into the sitting room and turn on the television. *Good*, he thought. *Maybe that will put him in a better mood.*

But it didn't. A second later, there was another snort of rage.

'What's up?' Mrs Hunter called.

'The television's useless!' Harvey shouted back. 'It's supposed to be the news. But there's nothing on except silly game shows. *Everything's* weird!'

'Oh, stop moaning!' Lloyd said. He sighed and went into the front room. 'There's bound to be news on BBC One.'

He picked up the remote control and flipped to Channel One.

But Harvey was right. There was no news on there. Instead, there were five people dressed up as penguins, trying to squeeze into a telephone box.

'Why do you want the news, anyway?' Lloyd said.

'I want to know about the football.'

Mrs Hunter heard that. She came in, pulling a face. 'That'll be in the paper tomorrow. If it's anything like today's paper. That's *all* sport.'

'Better than game shows,' Lloyd said in disgust. 'There's another one coming up now.'

The title was already spreading across the screen.

YOUR WILDEST DREAMS!!!!!

'Maybe there's something on the teletext,' Harvey said.

Picking up the remote control, he punched the button. The picture disappeared, but they could still hear the voice of the presenter on *Your Wildest Dreams.*

'*In a minute, we'll find out what happened to Philip Murphy when his WILDEST DREAM came true!!! But first, let's swirl the Dream Machine to pick out the name of our next lucky person. Surname first . . .* '

Lloyd barely heard it. He was staring in disbelief at the page of teletext. The whole screen was full of random characters, as if a monkey had been playing with a keyboard.

'That's hopeless!' he said.

Harvey groaned. 'Everything's falling to bits. The library's shut. The phones are wonky. We can't get on the internet. And now—no teletext and no proper television programmes or newspapers.'

'Oh, don't exaggerate,' Mrs Hunter said. 'No one's *making* you watch the television.'

She reached out for the remote control. As she did so, the unseen presenter of *Your Wildest Dreams* became even more manic.

'*So here it is, folks!! The magic moment. First we activate the left side of the Dream Machine. Ready, Gloria?*'

'Let's turn the whole thing off,' Mrs Hunter said impatiently.

She flicked back to the television picture, and her finger moved towards the *standby* button. But she didn't press it because, at that very instant, the surname card came whirling down the chute of the Dream Machine. Gloria pulled it out and held it up for everyone to see.

'*There it is!*' screeched the presenter. '*The magic surname is—Hunter!! So if that's your name, cross all your fingers and toes, because IT COULD BE YOU. Activate the other side, Gloria!*'

Harvey grabbed at the remote control. 'You

87

can't turn it off now, Mum! We've got to wait and see what the first name is. It might be me!'

'You wish!' Lloyd said scornfully. But he was watching too, and so was Mrs Hunter.

The Dream Machine went into action, with all its lights flashing. There was a loud fanfare, and Gloria picked up the first-name card.

'And the name is—'

Lloyd was holding his breath. Surely it couldn't be . . .?

'And the name is DINAH!' squeaked Gloria.

'Hello, Dinah Hunter!' bellowed the presenter. *'If that's your name, and you're under eighteen—start heading for the studio. If you get here before midday tomorrow, we'll make YOUR WILDEST DREAM come true!!!'*

Mrs Hunter began to dance round the room triumphantly. 'That's fantastic! Dinah's going to be so happy! You'll have to go and get her back, Lloyd. Her wildest dream!!'

Lloyd and Harvey looked at each other. Lloyd could see that they were both thinking the same thing.

It didn't feel right. Not in the middle of everything else that was going on.

It felt like danger.

9

Midnight Investigation

Mrs Barnes was watching *Your Wildest Dreams* as well, when Dinah and Michael arrived at Michael's house. She was so absorbed that she just nodded absent-mindedly when Michael asked if Dinah could stay the night.

'Course she can, dear. Do you want to come and watch this with me? It's really good.'

'Er . . . no thanks,' Michael said. He started shuffling away again.

Mrs Barnes looked past him. 'What about you, Deborah? Don't you want to see it?'

'Er . . . no thanks,' said Dinah politely. 'I—'

But Mrs Barnes had turned back to the television. Michael and Dinah crept out of the room and escaped upstairs.

'She's very *nice*,' Michael said. 'But she does watch television most of the time. And I couldn't bear to sit there. Not when I don't know if Dad's OK.'

'Of course not,' Dinah said briskly. 'We can't waste time, anyway. We ought to be hunting for clues.'

'But where can we look? It's too early to go to the AIU.'

'Where does your dad work when he's at home?'

'This is his study.' Michael pushed the door open. 'But I don't know if there's anything—'

Dinah stepped into the study and looked around. She'd been picturing an untidy room full of books, with piles of paper everywhere, but she was wrong. There were books all right—arranged on long shelves, in alphabetical order—but there were no papers at all. Only a bare desk with a computer.

'He keeps everything on the computer?'

'Sort of,' Michael said. 'Most of it's on the university computer—the one that's part of the Hyperbrain. This one's linked to it.'

'You mean—we can access the Hyperbrain from here?'

Michael nodded. 'That's how Dad did all his routine work. There's only personal stuff on this computer. Like his diary and the household records.'

Dinah looked thoughtful. 'His diary might be useful. Can you get into it?'

Michael hesitated.

'I don't think it's snooping,' Dinah said gently. 'Not if we really need to find him.'

Slowly, Michael sat down at the desk and switched on. The moment he began clicking the mouse, he started to relax. Dinah could see that he knew his way around the files. *He must have spent a lot of time in here with his dad*, she thought.

90

'There you are!' he said, after a moment. 'That's the diary.'

It was open at the beginning of the previous month. The entries were brief, and they were all about the Hyperbrain Conference. Tim Dexter's mind had obviously been buzzing with details:

Tues 13th 10.30—Phone Hamburg re HBC. Helmut J. to speak?
Wed 14th p.m. —See Claudia re HBC. Display Molecular Storage Units?
Fri 16th a.m. —Phone caterers. See Peter Giles
Thurs 22nd 09.30—BBC to discuss filming.

'Who are these people?' Dinah waved a hand at the screen.

Michael leaned forward to look over her shoulder. 'Helmut Jaeger's a professor at Hamburg. Peter Giles is one of Dad's research students—he's done a lot of work on the Hyperbrain—and you know who Claudia is.'

'Fine.' Dinah scrolled down. The entries went on and on, each one carefully dated. Then suddenly, about two days before the conference, the style changed. There was a single, undated entry, written across the screen.

The Controller will speak first.
Curiosity is the curse of the human brain.

91

The rest of that screen was blank.

Dinah shuddered. 'Scroll down again. Quickly.'

She was hoping for some information about what had happened at the Conference, but there was nothing like that. The next entries were very brief—and she couldn't understand a word of them.

Tues   2nd   —Submit report on DiBrAc to Hyperbrain
Wed   3rd   —Hyperb: more DiBrAc info by 6p.m.
Thurs 4th   —2p.m. Hyperb needs DiBrAc data.

Dinah frowned. 'What's DiBrAc?'

Michael shook his head. 'Haven't got a clue. Dad never mentioned it to me.'

'Do you think it had anything to do with the Hyperbrain?'

'It must have done. All Dad's work was linked to that. But I haven't got a clue what it means. Let me see what else I can find.'

Michael clicked away again and the screen changed, filling with notes and calculations. Dinah squinted at them, her brain whirring.

'I've never seen anything like *that* before.'

'No one has.' Michael gave her a quick grin, over his shoulder. 'This is all Dad's stuff about the new interface. The one that will let people talk directly to the Hyperbrain without a keyboard or a mouse or anything.'

92

'Sounds fantastic. Is there anything else about it?'

'Probably. You take a look.' Michael slid off the chair so that Dinah could sit at the desk.

She began to work her way methodically through Tim Dexter's files. Most of them seemed simple enough to understand, but the interface files baffled her.

'They don't add up. It's like trying to do a jigsaw with half the pieces missing.'

'That's because Dad had all the key bits in his head. There were some things he didn't tell anyone, not even people like Peter Giles. He said that spies could hack into the computer, but no one could steal his research without getting direct brain access.'

Dinah grinned. 'Direct access to a human brain?' she said. 'I don't suppose we'll ever—'

And then the words exploded in her mind. *Direct Brain Access. Direct Brain Access.*

DiBrAc.

She had to bite her lip to stop herself saying it out loud. The entries from Tim Dexter's diary were roaring through her memory.

Tues   2nd   —Submit report on DiBrAc to Hyperbrain
Wed   3rd   —Hyperb: more DiBrAc info by 6p.m.
Thurs 4th   —2p.m. Hyperb needs DiBrAc data.

'What's the matter?' Michael said, looking at her face.

Dinah didn't dare tell him what she was thinking. She made herself flip through a few more pages of equations before she answered. Trying to sound offhand.

'Nothing's the matter. I was just wondering— d'you think it will *ever* be possible? Direct Brain Access, I mean.'

Michael frowned. 'Dad said there *might* be a way. By diverting the electrical discharges in a person's brain. But it's too dangerous to use. No one knows what sort of damage it would cause.'

Abruptly, Dinah exited from the file she was in. 'I don't think we're going to find anything here,' she said quickly. 'Let's think about tonight. How are we going to get into the AIU?'

'You are staying?' Michael said anxiously.

'Of course.' There was no way she was letting him go in there on his own. Especially not with what she was thinking about DiBrAc. 'Can I have another go at phoning my mum?'

Michael picked up the phone from beside the desk and handed it to her. But when she dialled, there was nothing except a loud crackling noise.

Just before midnight, they sneaked through the

campus to the AIU building. There were groups of students wandering about, talking and laughing, but no one took any notice of Dinah and Michael.

'Thank goodness for *normal* students,' Dinah muttered. 'I saw some really weird ones the other day. They were—'

But Michael wasn't listening. He had reached the back door of the AIU and he was keying in the entry code.

'Be careful,' Dinah whispered.

Michael nodded, tapped the last number and pushed at the door. Immediately, a bell started ringing inside the building.

'Burglar alarm!' he hissed.

It sounded terrifyingly loud, but he didn't hesitate. He raced through the door and across the hall, to turn off the bell. Dinah went after him. Even in the dark, she could see the notice on the closed door of the first office. *Controller.*

'Are you sure there's no one here?' she whispered.

Michael put a finger to his lips and they stood dead still, holding their breath. The alarm hadn't sounded for more than a split second, but anyone in the building would have heard it.

No one came.

After three or four minutes, Dinah relaxed. 'All right. Where are we going to look?'

95

'Everywhere,' Michael said. 'Let's start with the offices.'

He pushed open the door of the Controller's office. Cautiously, Dinah stepped in after him as he flicked on the light.

It was very tidy and almost bare, except for a filing cabinet in one corner and a computer on the desk. Michael raced across to look in the filing cabinet and snorted with disgust.

'There's nothing in here except a video.'

'A *video*?' Dinah went to look over his shoulder. Why would the Headmaster be watching a video?

It was impossible to tell what it was. There was no label on the black plastic of the cassette, or on its box. Impatiently, Michael dropped it back in and pushed the drawer shut.

'There's nothing here. Let's look in the others.'

But the other offices were the same. Tim Dexter's had a bookshelf on one wall and a filing tray full of letters waiting to be answered, but otherwise it was as bare as the Controller's room.

'How about the lab?' Dinah said.

Michael marched over and threw the door open. The lab was bigger than the offices, but it was almost as empty. On the right hand wall was a row of shelves crowded with small pieces of equipment. The rest of the room was bare except for the big computer that dominated the room. The screen on the far wall was dull and blank, but Dinah could hear a low, continuous hum.

'Is that it?' she whispered. 'The Hyperbrain?'

'The bit that's here,' Michael said. 'But there are bits all over the world, of course.'

Dinah walked further into the room. There was a small video camera mounted in one corner, and it swivelled disconcertingly as she moved. She glanced up at it, thinking of the one she had seen in the Biogenetic Research Centre.

'Is that a security camera?'

Michael shook his head. 'Not exactly. It's part of the Hyperbrain Input System.'

'You mean . . . the Hyperbrain's watching us?'

Michael shrugged. 'I suppose so. But it's got information pouring in from all over the world. It's not likely to notice us.'

'I suppose not.' But Dinah didn't like it. She wandered over to the shelves. On the bottom shelf was a stack of dull grey cylinders. 'Oh look. These are the things Claudia invented, aren't they? Molecular Storage Units.'

Michael nodded and came to join her. 'Dad was really excited about those. He said they could store as much information as a human brain. He thought—' Suddenly he frowned and leaned forward. Moving the top Storage Unit, he took out the one underneath.

97

It wasn't dull grey like the others. It was translucent and glittering, as though it had been lit up from inside.

'What's happened to that?' Dinah said.

'I don't know. Unless it's been used.' Michael's frown deepened, and he began turning over the other things on the shelf. 'Someone's done something to this headband too.' He picked it up. 'This is what Dad used for brain mapping. He studied how people's brains worked, when he was designing the Hyperbrain.'

'And the headband's been altered?' Dinah said.

Michael nodded uneasily. 'I don't like it. I don't understand what's been going on in here.'

Dinah was horribly afraid that she did understand, but she didn't say so. She wasn't going to frighten Michael unless she had to.

'Could we . . . find out?' she said. 'Whatever the Headmaster's done, he'll have used the Hyperbrain, won't he? Can we get into it?'

'Maybe,' Michael said cautiously. 'But would you know what to ask?'

I hope not, Dinah thought. But she knew she had to try. 'I'll have a go,' she said. 'If you show me how to log on.'

'Sure.' Michael went across to the keyboard and tapped in some entry codes. He was answered not by a display on the screen, but by a computer voice.

'*What is your name?*'

He beckoned Dinah across. 'You answer,' he whispered. 'Just say your name.'

She was a bit startled, but she gave her name, in a clear, precise voice. 'Dinah Hunter.'

There was a noise above her head. Glancing up, she saw the camera on the ceiling swivelling towards her.

'*Wait for face identification,*' said the computer voice.

She blinked. 'What's going on?'

'It's the security check. Hyperbrain won't let you in until it's recognized you.'

'*Recognized* me?' But it's never seen me before.'

'It's not a person,' Michael said impatiently. 'Think of all the information it can get at— passport photos, newspaper files, all sorts of stuff. It's bound to have a picture of you somewhere, even if it's only a school photo.'

'Oh, great.' Dinah groaned. 'And it'll find that?'

'Now it's got your name. It's standard security procedure.'

He was still speaking when a grey, grainy picture began moving across the screen. He waved his hand at it.

'There you are. It hasn't just got a picture of you. It's got a video.'

Dinah stared. 'But how? What is it?'

Then another person stepped into the picture, and she knew what she was looking at.

'It's the Headmaster!' She whisked round to Michael. 'This must be the security video from where he was before. The place where Claudia got the creeper. Someone from the army took us in to get samples, and he was really worried because that video had disappeared. The Headmaster must have taken it.'

'And brought it here,' Michael said softly. 'You were right, Dinah. That *is* the Controller.'

'And if he's seen that video—he knows who I am.' Dinah took a long, deep breath. 'I think I ought to get out of here.'

But before she could even turn round, a voice spoke from behind them. A voice as smooth as syrup.

'What are you doing in here?'

For one, sick second, Dinah thought it was the Headmaster. Then she realized that it was a woman's voice.

There was a strange woman standing on the far side of the lab. She was tall and slim, with dark hair pulled into a heavy bun. Her hands were pushed into the pockets of her dark green lab coat. There was something disturbing about her stillness and the steadiness of her eyes.

Taking one hand out of her pocket, she pointed

at them with a long, pale finger. 'This is no place for children.'

'Who are you?' Michael said. 'What are *you* doing here?'

In the silence, the computer behind Dinah hummed more loudly for a moment. The woman said, 'I am connected to the Hyperbrain. I work here.'

Michael's eyes brightened, and he took a step forward. 'Do you know where my dad is, then?'

'He is not here,' the woman said. 'He has not been here for two days.' There was no trace of sympathy in her voice—and no trace of curiosity.

Dinah shuddered. 'Come on, Michael. We're not going to find anything here.'

She thought they would be shepherded out of the building, but the woman didn't move. She stood in her corner, watching them go. And, on the ceiling, the video camera swivelled, watching them too.

'How did she get in?' Dinah hissed, as they went out.

'Haven't got a clue. Never seen her before.'

'But she knew you.'

Michael stopped and stared. 'What do you mean?'

'When you asked about your father, she knew who you meant.'

Michael didn't answer, but Dinah saw his hands shaking as he closed the door behind them.

As they walked away up the hill, towards Michael's house, she glanced over her shoulder. There were no lights in the AIU now, but she was sure she glimpsed a dark shape at the window.

A dark shape with white hands that glimmered in the shadows.

102

10

Hiding Dinah

Lloyd woke up very early the next morning. The moment he opened his eyes, he thought, *I hope Dinah phones soon.* He was desperate to know whether she and Michael had managed to sneak into the AIU.

At eight o'clock, the phone rang, and he came rattling down the stairs, but his mother beat him to it. By the time he got there, she was shaking the phone and looking annoyed.

'There really is something wrong with this,' she said. 'I spent hours last night trying to phone Claudia, to tell Dinah about *Your Wildest Dreams*, but all I got was crackling. And now there's someone trying to get through to us, and I can't make out a word. Listen.'

Lloyd listened, but all he could hear was a noise like gargling underwater. Before he could decide what to do, the person at the other end gave up and rang off.

Mrs Hunter frowned. 'We'll have to get someone to look at the phone.'

'I don't think it's just *our* phone,' said Lloyd. 'I think there's something wrong with the whole system. All over the country.'

'Don't be silly. It's been going on for days. We'd have seen something in the papers. There's nothing about telephones.'

Mrs Hunter tossed the morning paper across the room. Lloyd caught it and looked down at the headlines. There certainly wasn't anything about telephones:

Great-gran celebrates 100th birthday
Conservatives slam Labour promises
Weather still dry

He turned the pages. 'There's no real news at all. Don't you think *that's* weird, too?'

Mrs Hunter started to laugh. 'Oh, Lloyd! What are you trying to say? That there's some kind of conspiracy?'

She picked up the phone and dialled, but it was no better. After a moment or two, she put it down in disgust.

'It's ridiculous! Dinah can't miss out on her wildest dream, just because the phone's not working. I'll have to go and get her.'

'No, I'll go,' Lloyd said quickly. 'Harvey and the others can come too.'

'*Would* you?' Mrs Hunter looked relieved. 'It would be a big help. I've got the plumber coming this morning.'

'No problem.' Lloyd gave his mother an angelic smile.

104

He didn't think Dinah should go anywhere near the *Wildest Dreams* studio, but he was delighted to have an excuse to go and see her. He had to find out what had happened.

Three quarters of an hour later, Lloyd and Harvey were setting out for the university with Ian and Mandy. Ingrid had refused to come.

'I promised to go to the café. Kate and I are going to try and get some more news on Crazyspace.'

Mandy pulled a face at her. 'It'll take hours to get anything. The phones still aren't working properly.'

'We'll try and try and try once more,' Ingrid rapped back at her. 'We've got to beat the emerald paw!'

Her hand shot out towards Mandy's face, with all the fingers wriggling. Mandy jumped back with a shriek.

'Don't! That's creepy!'

'The Green Hand *is* creepy,' Ingrid said. 'That's why Kate and I are staying with the chat. We want to get in touch with Plum and Jelly again, to find out why they've got so many badges at that Outdoor Centre.'

'Good idea,' said Lloyd. 'You concentrate on that, and we'll go and find out what Dinah and Michael have discovered.'

'And see how Dinah feels about having her name picked by the Dream Machine,' said Ian.

'The Dream Machine picked out *what*?' Dinah said.

She and Michael were in Tim Dexter's study, doing something on the computer. Mrs Barnes had sent the others up to join them, and Lloyd hadn't wasted any time getting to the point.

Dinah spun round on the computer chair and stared at him in amazement.

'It picked out your name,' Lloyd said. 'Dinah Hunter. If you go to the studio before midday, they'll make your wildest dream come true.'

Dinah went white. 'It's the Headmaster, isn't it? He's trying to get me.'

'But you said he wouldn't know who you were.' Harvey looked accusingly at her. 'You said he wouldn't remember.'

'I thought he wouldn't,' Dinah said, in a shaky voice. 'But I was wrong. He's got that security video from the Research Centre. It shows me talking to him, so he's seen my face, and he knows we've met.'

'Are you sure?' Lloyd said.

Dinah nodded 'Can we show them, Michael? Can you get into the Hyperbrain from here?'

Michael nodded. 'Easy. Just keep out of sight.

If I request a link with the Hyperbrain, that'll activate the video eye up there.'

'What on earth's that?' Lloyd said.

Dinah explained, as she ducked out of sight. 'It's so the Hyperbrain can recognize him. He has to give his name, and then it finds a picture of his face and checks it's the same person.'

'So you couldn't log in if you forgot your name?' Harvey said.

Ian patted him on the head. 'Don't worry. We know you find it hard to remember things.'

Harvey growled at him—and then stopped to grin as Michael's school photograph appeared on the screen. 'Brilliant picture, Mike!'

Michael blinked, as if he didn't quite understand the joke. Then he typed a request into the computer. '*Picture of Dinah Hunter?*'

He was online to the Hyperbrain now, and it responded immediately.

YOU ARE NOT MY MASTER, BUT I WILL CO-OPERATE WITH THIS REQUEST.

'What does that mean?' Dinah looked at Michael.

'Don't know.' He pulled a face. 'It's not supposed to have a master. Dad said it was going to co-operate with anyone who asked.'

Dinah and Lloyd glanced at each other, but they didn't say anything. Michael didn't notice because, at that moment, the screen filled with a picture of Dinah, standing straight and defiant. And facing her, looking icily furious, was the Headmaster. The images were grey and fuzzy, but they were perfectly recognizable.

Lloyd shuddered. 'That's where the Headmaster got your face from, then. But if *Your Wildest Dreams* is something to do with him he must know your name as well.'

'I suppose Claudia told him,' Dinah said miserably. 'It's lucky I forgot to give her our new address, or she would have brought him—' She stopped, choking.

Mandy squeezed her hand. 'It's not Claudia's fault. You know it isn't. He made her tell him.'

'But how did he know she knew?' Lloyd bit his lip. 'Has he ever seen you together, Di?'

Dinah thought about it. 'I don't see when he could have done.'

'He's been spying!' Harvey said shrilly. 'He's going to kidnap Di, isn't he? She'll vanish for ever, like Michael's dad!'

There was a little, soft gasp from Michael. Lloyd glared at Harvey.

'Don't be such a pinhead! Michael's dad hasn't vanished for ever. And Dinah's not going to vanish either.'

'She is in danger though,' Mandy said.

Lloyd nodded. 'We ought to get her out of the way for a bit. But where can she go?'

108

He looked round at them all. Everyone stared back blankly.

Then Ian's face brightened. 'She can come with Dad and me.'

'What?' Dinah said.

'On the lorry! Dad's going to Manchester today. I've often been with him, and he's always on at me to bring a friend.'

Lloyd beamed. 'That's great. The Headmaster'll never track Di down if she's in a lorry. How long can you keep her away?'

'Till tomorrow, probably. When Dad goes to Manchester, he usually stays the night with Gran on the way back.'

'And Di could go too?'

'No problem. Gran's got fourteen grandchildren. She's always having unexpected visitors.'

'Brilliant!' Lloyd beamed. 'Can you catch your dad before he goes?'

Ian looked at his watch. 'I reckon. If we shift a bit.'

'Go on then.' Lloyd gave Dinah a push. 'We'll sort things out here.'

Dinah hesitated. 'It seems like running away.'

'Don't be stupid!' Mandy said. 'We'll investigate much better if we haven't got to worry about you.'

'Yes I know, but—' Dinah was still reluctant.

It was Ian who worked out a way to persuade

her. 'Hey!' he said. 'Isn't that Outdoor Centre near Manchester? The one where Plum and Jelly are?'

'That's right!' Mandy said excitedly. 'You could get your dad to drop you off near it—say you're going for a walk or something. And you could go and investigate.'

'Great!' Lloyd grinned at her. 'See if you can find out why they've got so many badges, Di.'

'But . . .' Dinah was still hesitating. 'I haven't got the right shoes for walking. And suppose it rains—'

'You'll be fine in your trainers,' Lloyd said firmly. 'And you can take Mandy's waterproof.' He snatched it up, without bothering to ask Mandy, and pushed it into Dinah's hands. 'Go *on!*'

Grabbing Dinah's shoulders, he spun her round and Ian seized her arm, pulling her out of the room. The others stood and listened to the footsteps as the two of them went downstairs and out of the house.

When the front door closed, Michael shuddered. 'I wish we knew what was going on. I still don't understand why the Controller wants to get hold of Dinah.'

'It's not for any *good* reason,' Harvey said grimly.

Mandy nodded. 'He may be a clone, but he hasn't changed. He's grabbing all the knowledge and—'

110

Her voice stopped, suddenly. Something on the computer screen had caught her eye.

'What's the matter?' Lloyd spun round.

Mandy didn't need to explain. He understood the moment he saw the odd, wobbly picture on the screen. It was jerking around like a shot from a hand-held camera, but there was no mistaking the people it showed.

It was Dinah and Ian. They were standing by the bus stop, on the edge of the university campus. Suddenly, Ian pointed up the road and said something. Lloyd couldn't make out the words, but he heard the noise as a bus pulled in to the kerb.

'I don't understand,' Mandy said. 'That must be happening now! But how——?'

Dinah and Ian stepped into the bus and it pulled away. Almost immediately, another bus drew up in its place and the shot they were watching changed suddenly. All at once, they were on the second bus, with the driver looking up at them. For an instant, they saw two hands come forward, holding out money and reaching for a ticket.

Harvey blinked. 'What's going on? Is it a camera? How can he be holding it?'

The next moment, the shot changed again. Now they were looking at another part of the university altogether, about half a mile away. There didn't seem to be any connection with the first lot of

111

shots, except that there was the same kind of bumpy movement.

'What's the computer doing?' Mandy said. 'Where are these pictures coming from?'

'Straight out of the Hyperbrain.' Michael was looking puzzled too. 'People must be walking round with digital cameras. Radioing the pictures straight back to the Hyperbrain. Did you see anyone like that when you came in?'

Mandy shook her head. 'We didn't really see anyone at all. Only a group of weird students—'

'That's it!' Lloyd said. It came to him suddenly, in a horrible flash. When the others turned to look at him, he couldn't see why they hadn't realized too. 'Those weird students all looked the same— *and they were all wearing Green Hand badges!*'

'So?' Harvey said.

'So that's what the badges are for! *They're miniature cameras, spying for the Hyperbrain!* That's how the Headmaster found out that Claudia knows Dinah. He must have seen Di, through Claudia's badge.'

Michael gasped. 'You mean that's why Claudia came hunting for Dinah? Because he told her to?'

Mandy turned pale. 'But that's terrible!'

'Why?' Lloyd said.

The others turned to look at her. Her eyes were round and frightened.

112

'We sent Di away to keep her safe,' she whispered,
'. . . and we've just made things worse! She's going
to the Outdoor Centre, isn't she? And there are
hundreds of badges there!'

11

Plum and Jelly

Dinah and Ian had no idea that they were travelling into danger. Ian's father was delighted to have company. He even found them a couple of maps to help with their walk.

But he was rather puzzled about why they wanted to do it.

'You sure you really mean it?' he said, as they drew near to the drop-off point. 'It looks like rain. Why not stay in the lorry and come to Manchester?'

'We'll be fine,' said Ian. 'We've got waterproofs. And those sandwiches you bought us.'

Dinah nodded. 'And there's loads of time. We can have a couple of hours at the Outdoor Centre before we need to start back.'

Ian's father swung the wheel as they went round a corner. 'So who are these friends you're going to see?'

'They . . . er . . . ' Dinah had been hoping he wouldn't ask that. What could she say? *We've never met them, but their Crazyspeak names are Plum and Jelly?* 'They're very keen on computers, and—'

Luckily, at that moment, someone cut in front

of them, dangerously close. Ian's father braked and flashed his lights and by the time he'd finished saying what he thought about careless drivers he had forgotten his question.

Just before the next crossroads, there was a service area. He pulled in there and Dinah and Ian slid out of the cab.

'Thanks a lot, Dad!'

'We'll meet you back here this evening,' said Dinah.

Ian's father nodded. 'Don't be too late. We want to get to Gran's in time for one of her amazing meals.' He grinned and drew away, waving his hand.

Dinah looked at Ian. 'Off we go, then.' She hadn't got a clue what they were going to find at the Outdoor Centre.

Nor had Ian. 'Into the unknown! And keep your eyes peeled for Green Hand badges!'

There were plenty of badges around. They walked through three little villages on their way and, by one o'clock, they had seen at least six. One was on a postman who was emptying a postbox, three were on drivers going in the opposite direction, and two were on village shopkeepers, peering through their shop windows.

Both the shops had scrawled notices outside.

Sorry, no Advertiser this week

'That'll be the local paper,' Dinah muttered. 'Those are disappearing too, are they?'

'So's the library.' Ian nodded across the road at the sign sellotaped to its door:

Closed until further notice.

Dinah shuddered. 'It's the same everywhere, isn't it?' She stopped and pulled out the map. 'We go on another footpath now, round behind the church.'

The footpath went through some trees and up a hill. Towards the top of the hill, it turned right, to run along a fence. Dinah studied the fence.

'If we want to get in secretly, we've got to climb that.'

'We can do it along there. There's a stile.' Ian stepped off the path and through the rhododendron bushes.

They climbed the stile and went on to the top of the hill. Ian stopped in a clump of trees.

'That building down there must be the Outdoor Centre. If we eat our lunch here, we can watch it for a bit and decide what to do.'

'Good idea.' Dinah flopped down under the tree

116

and pulled on Mandy's waterproof. 'I wish I'd had time to go home and get some proper shoes. My feet are really sore.'

'Having a few blisters is better than getting caught by the Headmaster,' Ian said grimly.

'I know.' Dinah leaned back against the tree and unwrapped her sandwiches. 'What do you think he wants?' She took a bite and stared thoughtfully down the hill.

'Maybe—' Ian began.

But he didn't get any further. Dinah leaned forward and grabbed his arm.

'Look at that!'

'Ouch!' Ian pulled his arm away and rubbed it. 'No need to be violent!'

'Sorry, but I thought I saw —yes, look. There it is again.'

Dinah pointed across the valley to the trees on the opposite hill. There was a sudden flash of light. And then another.

Ian shrugged. 'It's just the sun reflecting off something.'

'Of course it is!' Dinah said impatiently. 'Someone's got a mirror. But can't you see the pattern in the flashes? *Look*. Short, long, long. Short, long. Long. Long, short, long, short.'

Still watching, she pulled out her pocket notebook and began to write down what she could see.

.－－/.－/－/－.－./....../－－－/...－/－/
.－－./－－－/.../....././－.－.－./－－－/－－/..../－.－./－－./

After the first few dots and dashes, Ian started looking interested. The moment the flashing stopped, he grabbed the pen and began to write letters underneath the marks Dinah had made.

.－－/.－/－/－.－./....../－－－/...－/－/
w a t c h o u t
.－－./－－－/.../....././－.－.－./－－－/－－/..../－.－./－－./
p o s s e c o m i n g

'Morse code,' he said.

Dinah still didn't understand. 'But what does it mean? *Watch out posse coming*. What posse?'

'Perhaps we ought to ask *them*,' Ian said softly.

He pointed down the slope in front of them and Dinah peered through the trees. A little way down the hill there were two figures huddled together whispering. Putting his finger to his lips, Ian began to crawl towards them and Dinah followed, keeping under cover of the rhododendron bushes.

When they got closer, Dinah could see that the two figures were a boy and a girl. The boy had a book in his hand, and he was calling out letters.

'S. S again. E.'

The girl was writing the letters on a piece of paper. As she copied the last one down, she sighed. 'We're so *slow*. We'll never be fast enough to pass on long messages.'

118

'Don't be so soft. We've got to do something now the telephone's packed up. And we're getting faster all the time.' The boy bent down and pulled the paper out of her hand. '*Watch out posse coming,*' he read.

Dinah took a step closer, to hear what he said next—but she wasn't careful enough about where she put her feet. There was a rustle of leaves, and a twig snapped.

The girl jumped, nervously. 'There's someone watching us!'

'OK, Jen. Don't panic.' The boy raised his voice. 'We know you're there. Who are you?'

Dinah looked at Ian and shrugged. Feeling rather stupid, they crawled out from behind the bush.

'We weren't really spying,' Dinah said. 'We just wanted to know about the message.' She smiled.

The boy didn't smile back. 'Take off your waterproofs,' he said sharply.

Dinah pulled off the waterproof she was wearing, feeling uneasy. The boy was looking at her in an odd way, scanning the front of her jacket. And so was the girl. What—?

Then their eyes switched to Ian's sweatshirt— and Dinah understood.

'You're looking for Green Hand badges!'

'I—' The girl looked anxious and took a step backwards.

119

'It's all right,' Dinah said quickly. 'We haven't got them!'

'We don't want them, either,' growled Ian. 'We hate what's going on.'

'Like?' the girl said cautiously.

'Like libraries closing!' said Dinah.

'Television news vanishing!' Ian said.

'Phones not working.'

'No decent newspapers!'

'The internet packing up!'

'Teletext going crazy!'

'Faxes going bananas.'

The boy and the girl looked wary. Dinah racked her brain for something that would make them trust her and Ian.

It was Ian who found it. Suddenly, he grinned and held out his hand. 'I know who you are! You're Plum and Jelly, aren't you?'

'We . . . ' The boy hesitated.

'We've come looking for you,' Ian said eagerly. 'We're Boff and ManUfan.'

It was like magic. The boy beamed and grabbed Ian's hand. 'That's right! I'm Paul, and this is my sister, Jenny. But what are you doing here?'

'We're investigating,' Dinah said. 'We want to know why you've got so many Green Hand badges round here. Is it a centre, or something?'

'It certainly is!' Paul said. 'Our father—'

Jenny grabbed at his hand. 'Not here!' she hissed. 'Remember there's a posse—'

She was too late. There was a sound of tramping feet coming up the hill towards them. Paul and Jenny shrank back towards the bushes, but there was nowhere to hide. They could only stand watching as a group of people came marching through the trees. There were a dozen of them, all around sixteen, and they were all wearing Green Hand badges.

When they saw Ian and Dinah they stopped and looked at them.

'They're our friends,' Jenny said quickly.

One or two of the posse smiled, but Dinah barely noticed. She couldn't stop staring at the glinting Green Hand badges pinned to their chests. She could see her own face reflected back towards her a dozen times, surrounded by the long, grasping fingers on the badge.

'Come on,' Jenny whispered. 'Let's get out of here.'

She pushed past the posse and led the way down the hill towards the Outdoor Centre, slipping between the rhododendron bushes to stay out of sight.

Dinah and Ian followed, with Paul. They had only moved a few yards when a man came out of the barn at the bottom of the hill. Dinah was sure they were invisible from where he was standing, but he headed up the hill, making straight for them.

Paul groaned. 'Oh no! He always comes out when there are people here. How does he know?'

They dodged sideways, into a copse of trees, but it was no use. The man strode up the slope and into their hiding place. He didn't bother to ask any questions. He just began to shout at Dinah and Ian.

'You're trespassing!'

A Green Hand badge glinted on the front of his jacket. Dinah didn't look at it. She was starting to hate the sight of them.

'They're not trespassing,' Paul said quickly. 'They're our friends.'

The man raised his eyebrows. 'Really?' His face was disbelieving. 'Suppose you tell me their names, then.'

'Yes. Um. Of course.' Paul looked helplessly sideways.

Ian jumped in to rescue him. 'I'm Ian.'

But the man didn't seem to be interested in him. It was Dinah he was staring at. 'How about the girl?' he said. 'What's her name?'

In the nick of time, Dinah realized what to do. 'I'm Mandy,' she said.

The man gave her a strange look. 'Are you sure?'

'Do you think I don't know my own name?' Coolly, Dinah held out the waterproof she had just taken off, turning it inside out to show the name sewn into the back of the neck.

Mandy's name.

The man read it and grunted. Without a word of apology, he pushed past Dinah and walked on, up the hill. A second later, they heard him giving instructions to the posse.

'You've got two hours to get to the places marked on your maps.'

There was a burst of muttering, and a girl's voice wafted down the slope. 'Can you tell us—?'

'You have enough information!' the man barked.

'But I can't help being curious—'

The answer came thundering down the hill. 'Curiosity is the curse of the human brain.'

Dinah caught her breath. Beside her, Jenny gave a little moan.

'Don't get upset, Jen,' whispered Paul. 'It must be an illness or something. You *know* Dad's not really like that!'

The horrible man was their father? Dinah felt almost as upset as Jenny. 'Don't worry!' she hissed fiercely. 'Paul's right. It's not his fault. It's got something to do with those Green Hand badges!'

Slowly, Jenny lifted her head, and she and Paul looked at each other. Paul nodded.

'That makes sense. Dad was fine until he got that badge.'

'Where did it come from?' said Ian.

Jenny glanced up the slope. Her father was still busy giving orders, but she lowered her voice anyway. 'He got it from a conference. He went to read a paper on physical and spatial intelligence. That's what he studies here.'

'What he *used* to study,' Paul said bitterly. He scowled. 'All he does now is dish out Green Hand badges to people and send them snooping round the villages in posses. Then they go back to their own towns. He's filling the whole country with Green Hands.'

'And you try and keep track of them?' Dinah said.

Jenny nodded. 'Edward helps us. He's our friend —the one you saw signalling—and his mother's a journalist. She went to report on the conference Dad went to, and she came back with a badge as well. Now she won't write about anything except gardens and cookery.'

'And if Edward asks a question . . . ' Jenny pulled a face and chanted. *'Curiosity is the curse of the human brain.'*

The posse above them was moving off now. Dinah looked up, watching everyone go. Seeing the Green Hand badges carried off in all directions.

'Does Edward's mother give out badges, like your dad?'

Paul shook his head. 'No, it's only Dad who does that. He came back from the conference with boxes of them.'

Dinah looked thoughtful. 'I'm sure they're the key to the whole thing. You couldn't get hold of one, could you?'

Paul and Jenny looked at each other. Then Paul stepped back and glanced up the hill. Their father was walking away from them, towards the stile.

Paul waited until he had climbed over. Then he said, 'OK.'

He went flying down the hill towards the Outdoor Centre, and Dinah took a step out of the rhododendrons, to see where he went.

As she did so, she saw another glint of light from the opposite hill. Jenny saw it too. Immediately, she pulled the notebook out of her pocket and started to note down the dots and dashes. Ian grinned at Dinah.

'It's a great system, isn't it? Who needs the internet?'

He was only joking, but Dinah almost stopped breathing.

'You're right! We don't need the internet. Or Crazyspace. We can keep in touch with people even if all those things collapse!'

SPLATweb

Crazyspace was certainly collapsing. Lloyd had spent most of the day in the internet café, and he was getting crosser and crosser.

'We *need* to tell people that the badges are spying on them. Can't you get it over to them, Ing?'

'I'm doing my best,' Ingrid said sulkily.

She'd certainly been working hard. Over and over again, she had typed in the same message.

Hands have ears and fists have eyes!
Badges can be snoopy spies!
They may bring danger too, I fear.
Don't let them see! Don't let them hear!

It had looked fine on the screen, and it should have made sense to the people who had chatted to them before. But it wasn't getting across—as far as they could tell from the messages they were getting back.

M $, is yo¶r c♥n↕ecti♥n b♥d!
Scr♥mbl↕d le♣♣ers ♥re re♥l¶y s♥d!

Michael stared gloomily at the screen. 'We're wasting our time, aren't we?'

For the tenth or eleventh time, the words flickered and disappeared and another message took its place.

LINE ERROR
CONNECTION LOST

It was a message they were getting sick of. Kate glowered at the computer.

'*Horrible* thing!' Ingrid said sulkily. 'I think it's teasing us!'

Lloyd grinned. 'It's not the Hyperbrain, you know.'

'Even the Hyperbrain hasn't got a sense of humour,' Michael said. His voice was thin and tense and he looked as though he hadn't had any sleep for three days now.

Ingrid pulled a funny face, trying to cheer him up.

'Can the Hyperbrain laugh like a drain?' she chanted.

'Can it make us laugh till we crack in half?

'Does it pass the time with a nonsense rhyme?

'Or give a little wriggle as it starts to giggle?

'Or—'

'Stop! Stop!' Lloyd put his hands over his ears. 'That would drive anyone mad. Even the Hyperbrain.'

Ingrid punched the air. 'That's the idea! It's our secret weapon. Ingrid's SLS!'

'Ingrid's *what*?' said Mandy.

'Special Laughter Service! Want to hear a joke?'

'No!' Lloyd put his hands over his ears. 'I can't bear it.' He nodded to Kate. 'Turn that computer off. There's no point in doing anything else tonight. We'll come back tomorrow morning and try again. Maybe Dinah and Ian will have some good ideas.'

'Good ideas?' Dinah said the next morning. 'I've got the *best* idea you've heard for years!'

Ian's father had dropped her and Ian off right outside the café and they had come running in, looking pink and excited.

'It's brilliant!' Ian said. 'But we need to try and tell people about it before Crazyspace packs up altogether.'

'We won't need it for long,' Dinah said. 'Because we're going to start a network of our own—'

'A SPLATweb,' interrupted Ian. 'With mirrors—'

'And torches—'

'And flags—'

'*Flags?*' Lloyd stared at them. Had they gone mad?

'Flags for semaphore!' Dinah said impatiently. 'Don't you see? It'll be faster than passing on news by post.'

'Safer, too,' Ian said. 'If we start getting sacks

128

full of letters, someone with a Green Hand badge is sure to notice. But they won't spot SPLATweb if it uses lots of different things.'

Lloyd hadn't quite got what they meant, but Michael understood. He jumped out of his seat.

'We could use homing pigeons, too! I know someone who has those.'

'Great!' Dinah grinned at him. 'And we can send messages with lorry drivers, like Ian's dad, and find people with CB radios—'

'I'm sure my uncle and his friend had those! They used to talk to people all over the country,' said Mandy.

'We need everything,' said Dinah. 'Anything. Then all we've got to do is set up the network. And we can use Crazyspace for that. No one's going to spot it, as long as we keep the messages sounding like nonsense.'

'Better hurry,' Lloyd said grimly. 'It's been going on and off all morning.'

Dinah sat down. 'Let's see if we can get a connection, then.'

'I'll do it.' Kate pulled her chair up to the computer. 'And Ingrid can tell me what to say. She's good at nonsense.'

Ingrid stuck out her tongue, but she didn't waste time arguing. As soon as Kate got the connection, she was ready to rap.

'Keep in touch with all your might
'Using flags and sounds and light.
'Pigeons, milkmen—any way
'To get your message here today.
'Flash it, squeak it, send a bird—
'Any way to get it heard.
'If you want the Green Hands gone,
'Get the news and pass it on!'

Everyone was leaning forward to watch the screen and wait for the answers.

Except Michael.

He was standing behind the others. Glancing back, Lloyd saw him staring at Dinah and Ian. His fists were clenched and he was biting his lip. Lloyd knew exactly what he wanted. The question in his mind was so clear he might just as well have been yelling it.

Have you seen my dad?

Lloyd nudged Dinah, and she understood the moment she looked round. She pulled her chair away from the others, so that she could talk quietly to Michael.

'We haven't got fantastic news,' Lloyd heard her say. 'But we have found out something. They give out Green Hand badges at the Outdoor Centre. Loads and loads of them.'

'We've even got one!' Ian said over his shoulder. 'Show them, Di.'

130

'*What?*' Lloyd jumped up in horror. 'You haven't—?'

'Oh yes we have.' Dinah was smiling. 'Look.' She put her hand into her pocket.

'No!'

Lloyd threw himself forward. As Dinah's hand came out of her pocket, he snatched the badge from her fingers. Then he grabbed Ian's waterproof, which was lying on the next table, and bundled it round and round, muffling the badge in as many layers as possible.

Dinah stared. 'What on earth are you doing?'

'You don't understand!' Harvey hissed. 'The badges are for spying on people. Mini cameras and microphones. They feed information back to the Hyperbrain.'

'*What?*' Dinah went white.

Michael nodded. 'We saw you on the screen, in Dad's study. When you and Ian got on that bus at the university, *we were watching you.*'

'What have you done since you got that badge?' Lloyd looked round wildly, half-expecting to see the Headmaster appear in the café. 'Has it picked up your face? And where you've been?'

Dinah shook her head slowly. 'No, it's been in my pocket all the time. But—' She sank into a chair and put her head in her hands.

'Don't worry,' Mandy patted her shoulder. 'It's not that bad.'

'Isn't it?' Dinah muttered. Lloyd couldn't see her face, but her voice was shaking.

'What's the matter?' he said.

Dinah lowered her hands. 'Don't you see?' she said. 'There are badges everywhere, pinned on to all sorts of people. And everything they see is being fed straight back to the Hyperbrain. The Head-master's beaten us, hasn't he?'

'Why?' Mandy said.

Dinah gave her a weary smile. 'If he's in control of the Hyperbrain, he's got all the information in the world. Everything that's on computers and in books, *and* everything that people can hear and see. And we've got nothing. We can't even phone each other. How can we possibly fight back?'

Lloyd had never seen her so near to giving up. He grabbed her arm and shook it. 'Don't be so feeble! We've got our own eyes and ears, haven't we? And we've got each other. We have to go on!'

Michael echoed him. 'We *have* to!' His voice was desperate.

Dinah clenched her fists. 'It's so awful not being able to find out anything. It's like . . . like being blindfolded.'

'Then find things out!' Lloyd said fiercely. 'People

didn't always have the internet. They didn't always have books. They just had to go out and see things for themselves. If we can't do anything else, we'll have to do that!'

Dinah stared down at her fists for a moment. Then she looked up. Her face was still pale, but it was determined now. 'You're absolutely right. That's what we've got to do. And that means I've got to go back to the university.'

'What?' Harvey almost shrieked.

Mandy was looking horrified too. 'You can't! The Headmaster's hunting for you, and he knows what you look like. It's much too dangerous.'

'So?' Dinah said. She stood up. 'I've got to find out what he's up to—and I'm not going to do that by sitting around here. You can set up the SPLATweb perfectly well without me.'

Lloyd looked at her. He knew he ought to argue. He knew she was stupid to be walking into danger like that. But—he knew she was right. If they were ever going to discover what the Head-master was planning, someone had to go to the university. And Dinah was the best person to go.

'Be careful,' he said.

Dinah nodded and picked up her bag. 'I will. And you get SPLATweb going, as fast as you can. I've got a feeling we're going to need it soon. Borrow those CB radios Mandy was talking about.

Find people who travel around a lot. Get Michael to talk to his friends about the pigeons.'

'I'm not staying to talk about pigeons,' Michael said quietly. He was scribbling an address on a piece of paper. 'This is where they are, Ingrid. Can you and Kate sort it out? I'm going with Dinah.'

Ingrid took the paper and grinned. 'Pigeons? No problem!'

Dinah looked at Michael for a second and then she nodded. 'OK. Come on.'

The two of them set off across the café. As they reached the door, Ingrid called after them.

'Hey! Di!' They both looked round and she waved. 'SPLAT for ever!'

'SPLAT for ever!' Dinah said gravely.

Then she and Michael went off together.

13

Not Just a Computer . . .

When Dinah and Michael reached the university, it was almost lunch time. It took them a long while to get near the AIU, because they had to keep dodging groups of weird students wearing Green Hand badges.

'We'll need a place to hide,' Dinah said. 'Is there somewhere we can watch the AIU without being seen?'

'There's a garden by the English Faculty building. I used to play at spying on Dad when I was little. And we had signals—' Michael's voice wobbled a bit, and he stopped.

Dinah could see how much he was missing his father. She wanted to tell him it was going to be all right, that Tim Dexter would come back and be the same as before, but there was no point in pretending. None of them knew what was going to happen.

'Let's go to the garden,' she said quickly. 'We'll watch who goes in and out of the Unit and see if we can work out anything from that. Where do we go?'

Michael led the way up the hill opposite. The

garden was tucked round one side of the English building and there was a bench where they could sit, shielded by a big rose bush. There was a wonderful view of the campus from there.

Dinah settled herself on the bench and took out her notebook. 'Let's make a note of everyone who goes in and out.' She handed the book to Michael. 'You'll recognize people. You write the names.'

She was pretty sure she would remember anything important, without writing it down, but the writing would give Michael something to do. That was better than sitting and fretting.

He took the book and turned to a clean page. Very neatly, he wrote two headings:

GOING IN   *COMING OUT*

Then they settled down to watch.

By five o'clock, their list was quite long:

GOING IN	*COMING OUT*
2 weird students	*1 weird student*
Claudia (with Molecular Storage Unit)	*Claudia (without Molecular Storage Unit)*
3 weird students	*2 weird students*
5 weird students	*4 weird students*
Green Hand van (unloading)	

Green Hand van (unloading)
2 weird students

Dinah pulled a face at it. 'It's not much help. I can't even tell which of those students are which. They all look the same to me.'

'Why do they keep going in and out?'

'The Headmaster must be giving them orders.'

'But what orders?' Michael twisted his fingers together miserably. 'And why did Claudia take in that Molecular Storage unit? What's going on?'

He twisted his fingers the other way, and the pencil snapped suddenly, with a dull crack. Dinah wished she knew how to cheer him up. Her mother would have hugged him and Mandy would have had something comforting to say, but she just felt helpless.

The only way *she* could help Michael was by trying to find his father. She frowned down at the list again—and this time she noticed something odd about it.

'We haven't seen that woman yet. The one we met in the lab. She said she worked with the Hyperbrain, but she doesn't seem to be around.'

'Maybe she's not here today.' Michael's eyes flicked up from the paper, towards the front door of the AIU. 'Or maybe—'

He broke off. Clutching at Dinah's sleeve, he

pointed to the door. A young man in jeans was walking out of the Unit, looking vague and distracted.

Dinah frowned. 'Who's that? Another weird student?'

Michael shook his head and stood up. 'It's Peter Giles! My dad's postgraduate student!' he said excitedly. 'He might know where Dad is!'

Nervously, Dinah scanned the windows of the AIU building. 'I think we ought to be careful—'

'You can be careful if you like! I want to talk to Peter!'

Dropping her arm Michael ran out of the garden and slithered down the slope towards the main path, calling as he went.

'Peter! Peter, wait for me!'

The young man didn't react at all. He just went on walking, in the same vague way, almost as if he were asleep. Michael slid down the last few feet to the path and landed right in front of him.

'Hi, Peter,' Dinah heard him say. 'Didn't you hear me? I—'

He stopped. The student was staring straight past him, with unfocused eyes.

'Peter? It's *me*. Michael Dexter. Don't you recognize me?'

There was no answer. Peter's face was completely blank. Michael stood staring at him in bewilderment.

Then the man in the brown anorak came hurrying out of the Unit. Ignoring Michael, he went up to Peter and put a hand on his shoulder. She couldn't hear what he said, but when he moved off Peter went with him, like a zombie.

Michael stood motionless, watching them climb into a car and drive off. Then he clambered up the slope, back to the garden. His face was white and frightened as he sat down on the bench again.

'That was horrible,' he whispered.

'He didn't know who you were?'

'He didn't know anything. It was like talking to someone—' Michael shuddered. 'Like talking to someone who wasn't *there*. His eyes—'

Dinah forgot about not being like her mother or Mandy, and put an arm round his shoulders.

'Don't worry. The Headmaster's terrible, but he's never won yet. We'll beat him! When we find out what's going on.'

'But that's just what we can't do!' Michael said. It was almost a wail. 'Every day it gets harder to find things out. All the knowledge is disappearing. And now—'

He stopped. Dinah could feel his whole body shaking.

'It's always worse if you keep things to yourself,' she said. 'What's really scaring you? Tell me.'

Michael spoke slowly, as if he had to force the words out. 'First the Hyperbrain was taking the knowledge out of libraries and newspapers and things. That was bad enough. Then we found it was using the Green Hand badges to snatch the knowledge from under people's noses—the things they actually see and hear. That felt much more dangerous. And now—'

'With Peter?' Dinah said.

Michael nodded. 'It's as if the Hyperbrain actually got inside his head and snatched the knowledge out. I think it's using—'

There was a long silence. Then he said three more words, speaking so softly that Dinah had to lean closer to hear.

'Direct Brain Access.'

Direct Brain Access, Dinah thought. *DiBrAc*. She was horribly afraid he was right. But she wasn't going to tell him that.

'You told me your dad wouldn't work on that! And you said no one knew how to do it!'

Michael twisted his fingers together. 'Maybe they do now. Maybe someone's worked it out.'

'Like who?'

'Like . . . the Hyperbrain.'

140

Dinah hadn't been expecting that. She stared. 'The Hyperbrain? By itself?'

'I keep telling you—it's not just a computer. It thinks, like us. It's curious and it wants to *know*.'

Dinah sat in silence for a moment, trying to work out what that meant. 'You're saying that it's the Hyperbrain itself that wants all this information?'

Michael nodded. 'I think so. I think it wants more and more and more. As if it can never be satisfied.'

'But why would the Headmaster let it grab everything? If he's in charge—'

'What makes you so sure he *is* in charge?' Michael said. He looked up, challenging her. 'How do you know the Hyperbrain hasn't outwitted him?'

Dinah felt as if a terrifying black space had opened up in front of her. She stared down at the AIU building and thought about the Headmaster and the Hyperbrain.

What was really going on in there?

14

Mrs Hunter Steps In

Lloyd and Harvey were trying to find out what was going on too. But they were doing it with mirrors.

They were at home, helping to set up SPLATweb's Morse Code Link. There was a chain of mirrors and flags and Lloyd was reading the flashes from one mirror—Mirror Three—and calling them out to Harvey, so that Harvey could wave his flags and pass the message on to Mirror Four.

.../_/.._/_/.._/_ _ _/_/..../_/_/.../_/_ _/_ _ _/_ _/..../_.../...

s t a t i o n h a s t w o g h b s

Harvey was getting flustered.

'I can't signal fast enough!' he grumbled, when there was a pause. 'Why can't we do something simpler? Like the CB radios or the pigeons? Or being in charge, at the internet café?'

Lloyd wasn't sympathetic. 'You'll get a turn. But we've got to start this going too. We need all the news we can get.' He frowned. 'I just wish we could hear something from Di.'

Harvey nodded. 'I thought you'd give her one of those CB radios.'

'What?' Lloyd stopped looking out of the window. He turned to stare at Harvey. 'Say that again.'

Harvey shrugged. 'Dinah could have had one of those CB radios, couldn't she? From Mandy's uncle. Why didn't you make her take one?'

'Because I didn't think of it, you dodo!' Frantically, Lloyd began to push his feet into his trainers.

'What are you doing?' Harvey said.

'I'm going to Mandy's, of course! To get a radio and take it to Di.'

'But it's almost tea time.'

'Danger doesn't stop for meals.' Scornfully, Lloyd banged out of the room. Harvey heard the front door slam behind him as he left the house.

Mrs Hunter called from upstairs. 'Was that Lloyd going out?'

'He . . . er . . . ' Harvey dithered.

'Where has he gone? It's a bit late.'

'Not . . . um . . . not really,' Harvey was floundering. As his mother came downstairs, he switched on the television, to distract her. 'Look, it's only just time for *Your Wildest Dreams*.'

They saw the screen twinkling with stars.

'Yes, folks!' said a fake-American voice. 'We're here show to you a dream come true! In just a few minutes, we'll be picking next week's lucky dreamer, but first let's meet the girl whose name was chosen last time.'

'What?' Mrs Hunter sat down abruptly on the couch. 'Is Dinah there after all?'

Harvey sat down too. *She can't be!* he was thinking. *She wouldn't go there*—

But it sounded as if she had.

'What a dreamer she is!' said the presenter's voice. 'You're going to love watching her favourite fantasy come true. Ladies and gentlemen, please give a big welcome to—'

No!

'—Miss Dinah Hunter!'

There was a terrifying pause. Trumpets blew a fanfare and Harvey gripped the arms of his chair, feeling sick.

Then a small, skinny figure marched on to the screen. She was wearing high heels and a very short mini-skirt and there was a large tattoo on her left arm. Her wild red hair was permed into a frizz.

'What on earth—?' Mrs Hunter said.

'It's the wrong Dinah Hunter!' Harvey was so relieved that he started laughing. And once he started, he couldn't stop. He rolled sideways on the couch, punching at the cushions.

Mrs Hunter was baffled. 'What's so funny? If

there's another Dinah Hunter, it means that *our* Dinah's missed out. Don't you care?'

'Yes, of course,' Harvey gasped. 'I . . . I—'

But he couldn't hold his giggles back. He kept imagining the Headmaster marching into the studio, thinking he'd caught the right Dinah Hunter. And then seeing—The thought of that set Harvey laughing again.

It was a bad mistake. Mrs Hunter lost her temper.

'You're all being very peculiar. Something's going on, isn't it? First Dinah goes off to the university and now Lloyd's walked out. I don't like it, and I'm not getting any sense out of you. I'm going to Claudia's to fetch Dinah back. *She'll* tell me what's up.'

That stopped Harvey's laughter. He sat up sharply. 'But you can't—! I mean—'

'No?' His mother gave him a long, hard look. 'Why not?'

'Because . . . I mean . . . ' The whole story flew through Harvey's mind, at top speed. He didn't see how he could ever explain. 'I mean . . . you can't go on your own,' he said at last. 'I'll come too.'

He didn't know what he was going to do, but at least he would be *there*.

* * *

145

Mrs Hunter drove on to the campus and parked in the multi-storey car park.

'All right,' she said. 'Now where's Claudia going to be? At home or in her office?'

'I'm . . . not sure,' Harvey stuttered. 'I know she works late sometimes but—'

Mrs Hunter was in no mood to hang around. 'We'll start in the Biological Sciences building, then.'

She strode out on to the campus and Harvey followed, frantically trying to slow her down. 'Look at those students, Mum! They're all exactly like each other! Look at their funny badges!'

It was useless. Mrs Hunter kept straight on, heading for the Biological Sciences building. Even when Harvey grabbed her arm, she didn't slow down. Sweeping into the building, she entered the lift, and pressed the button for the top floor. Harvey had to move quickly to get inside before the doors closed.

He stared out through the glass, wishing he could catch sight of Dinah. Or Lloyd. Or Michael. But the only person he saw was a thin man in a brown anorak, coming out of the Artificial Intelligence Unit.

When the lift reached the top, Mrs Hunter stepped out and knocked briskly on the door opposite, which had Claudia's name on it. Claudia opened the door.

146

Harvey was shocked by how stiff and unfriendly her face was. Mrs Hunter didn't seem to notice, though. She launched straight into a little speech she had obviously been planning.

'Hello, Claudia. Thank you for having Dinah to stay for so long. I was just passing, so I thought I'd come and pick her up.'

'You . . . what?' The stiffness vanished, and Claudia looked bewildered.

Mrs Hunter gave her a sharp glance. 'You don't remember me, do you? I'm Dinah Hunter's mother.'

The words had an amazing effect. Suddenly, Claudia stopped looking cold and distant, and a warm smile spread across her face.

'Mrs Hunter! Of course! How's Dinah? It seems ages since I saw her.'

'I'm sorry?' Mrs Hunter looked puzzled. Slowly she turned to Harvey.

'Honestly, Mum, I can explain—'

He was desperately trying to invent a sensible explanation when his eye caught a glint of green on Claudia's shirt. He froze, staring in horror.

He'd forgotten Claudia's Green Hand badge! Everything they said was going straight to the Hyperbrain. And the Headmaster.

Harvey grabbed his mother's hand. 'We mustn't waste time. Dinah's not here. She—'

But Mrs Hunter wouldn't be distracted. She shook him off and took a step nearer to Claudia. 'I don't understand. Didn't you phone up and ask Dinah to stay? Lloyd said she was at the university, so I assumed she was with you. If you haven't seen her—where is she?'

Inside his head, Harvey groaned. The Headmaster must be gloating! He'd probably caught every word of that. *Lloyd said she was at the university* . . . Now the Headmaster would know that Dinah was on the campus.

Where *was* she? Harvey peered over his shoulder, hoping, wildly, that she would appear. But he couldn't see anything much except the entrance of the Artificial Intelligence Unit, and Dinah wasn't going to pop up there. She'd promised not to go in. He sighed and started to turn back to his mother and Claudia.

And then he saw something that turned him icy-cold.

There was a figure in the doorway of the Unit. A tall figure with pale hair and dark glasses.

Harvey thought he was going to faint. He couldn't hear what his mother and Claudia were saying. He forgot they were there. He just stood staring down in horror.

It was *him*! The Headmaster. There was no mistaking that cold, stern face, and the scornful way it looked round at the campus. He was there—and he was just the same as before!

He wasn't on his own, either. A whole group of weird students with Green Hand badges had followed him out of the building. He was busy giving orders, sending them out in all directions.

What was he doing?

Harvey was trying to see, when Mrs Hunter shook his arm.

'Harvey? What's the matter?'

'I . . . er . . . nothing.' He gulped and turned round.

'I expect he's worrying about Dinah,' Claudia said calmly. 'But there's no need. She's probably with Michael Dexter. Come into my office and I'll try and get through to them.'

With a last backward glance at the Headmaster, who was walking away from the AIU building, Harvey reluctantly followed his mother into the office. Claudia picked up her telephone, dialled, and frowned.

'Not *again*! The phone's completely dead. We'll have to go over to the Dexters' house—'

She was interrupted by a flicker on the computer screen and she smiled apologetically.

'I'll just take a look at my e-mail.' She laughed. 'You never know. It might be Dinah.'

Harvey read the message over her shoulder.

Please send Mrs Hunter and Harvey to the AIU laboratory.

'That looks like the answer to your problem,' Claudia said. 'Dinah must be there.'

'Typical!' Mrs Hunter grinned. 'Trust her to find a lab!' She turned and headed out of the office. 'Just wait till I get hold of her! Come on, Harvey.'

'But—'

Harvey couldn't make sense of it. Dinah had *promised* not to go to the AIU. That message couldn't be from her. But it couldn't be from the Headmaster, either. He'd just walked away from the Unit.

So who *had* sent it?

There was no time to think about it. Mrs Hunter was getting impatient. 'Come *on*, Harvey. Do you know where we have to go?'

'I'll show you,' Claudia said. She walked out on to the landing with them, and pointed down at the AIU building. 'That's it. There's a security thing at the entrance. Buzz and give your name, and someone will let you in.' She waved them into the lift.

As they slid down towards the ground, Harvey stood staring out at the campus. He could still see the tall figure of the Headmaster in the distance, striding away from them. By the time the lift stopped, he was completely out of sight.

150

Harvey followed his mother out of the Biological Sciences building and across to the AIU. She was peering ahead, at the entrance.

'Did Claudia say there was a buzzer?'

It was beside the front door. Harvey pressed it, and his mother leaned forward ready to speak her name into the grille.

But no one asked her to. Instead, the door clicked open and a voice came out of the speaker. A woman's voice.

'Good afternoon, Mrs Hunter. Good afternoon, Harvey. Please come in, and walk through to the back of the building.'

Harvey looked at his mother. 'Funny voice,' he said. 'It's too—' But he couldn't find the right word.

'Everyone sounds odd through those things,' said Mrs Hunter briskly. 'Come on.'

Pushing the door open, she walked into the building. There were office doors on each side of them and straight ahead, on the far side of the entrance hall, was a door marked *Laboratory*. They walked towards it, and the woman's voice spoke again, from behind the door.

'Please come in, Mrs Hunter. We must discuss something to do with Dinah. Harvey can wait outside.'

'Don't go!' Harvey whispered. 'It doesn't feel right.'

'Don't be silly,' Mrs Hunter said. 'I won't be long.'

She pushed the door open and went in. Harvey peered over her shoulder, trying to catch a glimpse of the woman who had spoken, but he couldn't see anything except an armchair and a large computer screen.

'Please close the door,' the woman's voice said.

Mrs Hunter turned, gave Harvey a rather worried smile and shut the door behind her.

Harvey crept up and put his ear to the door. He heard the murmur of two voices, but he couldn't make out any words.

After about ten minutes, the voices stopped. He pressed his ear closer to the wood, straining to catch a sound, but all he could hear was his own hair rustling. And an odd movement of the air that wasn't really sound at all. More like a kind of tingling.

Then the woman's voice spoke again, loud enough for him to hear clearly. 'Come in, Harvey.'

He reached for the door handle, and found that his hand was shaking. Taking a deep breath, he pushed the door open and walked through. His mother was sitting in the armchair, with her back to him. He couldn't see anyone else in the room.

'Mum?' he said uncertainly.

She didn't turn round.

'Mum!'

The mocking voice that answered him came out of the empty air.

'You won't get her to speak to you. You're not clever enough to work out how . . .'

15

The Trap

At that very moment, Lloyd was racing across the campus to Michael's house. It had taken him ages to get the CB radio from Mandy, and then the bus had been late. He felt as if he'd never get to Dinah.

Even something as simple as crossing the campus was harder than usual. Everywhere he looked, there were weird students with Green Hand badges. They seemed to be stopping people and talking to them.

Lloyd dodged the first two, keeping out of sight of their badges, but the third one stepped in front of him, blocking his way.

'Excuse me,' he said. 'I'd just like to ask—'

Lloyd saw his own face, reflected very small in the student's badge. *Keep calm*, he told himself firmly. *The Headmaster won't recognize your face.* He forced himself to smile politely.

'Er . . . sorry. What did you say?'

'Excuse me.' The student repeated exactly the same words as before. 'I'd just like to ask whether you've seen this girl. She's somewhere on the campus.' He held out a sheet of paper.

Lloyd found himself staring at a grey, fuzzy picture of Dinah's face. He made himself study it for ten seconds or so before he looked up and shook his head. 'Haven't a clue.'

'Thank you,' the student said, mechanically.

He moved on down the path, towards the next person. As Lloyd began to run, he heard him start up again.

'Excuse me. I'd just like to ask whether you've seen . . .'

There was no time to waste! Lloyd tore through the campus, to Michael's house, and banged on the door.

Mrs Barnes opened it, looking startled. 'Yes, dear?'

'I . . . er . . . sorry. Is Michael—?'

'Up in the study. First door at the top of the stairs. Spends too much time with that computer, if you ask me.'

She waved Lloyd on, and he ran upstairs and knocked. There was a pause, and a shuffling noise. Then Michael opened the door. When he saw Lloyd, he grinned.

'It's all right, Dinah. You can come out. You're safe.'

Lloyd looked sharply at Dinah as she crawled out from behind the desk. 'You're *not* safe. The Headmaster's got his students out hunting for you. You mustn't go out.'

155

'But I've got to,' Dinah said impatiently. 'I won't find out anything in here.'

'It's not going to help if the Headmaster catches you. He—'

'Ssh!' Michael said suddenly.

The door bell was ringing again. They all heard Mrs Barnes shuffle to the door, and Lloyd pointed at the desk, meaning that Dinah ought to hide again.

But there was no chance of that. Before she could move, feet came running up the stairs and someone flung the door open. A frantic voice shouted at them all.

'You've got to help! It's Mum!'

Dinah had never seen Harvey so distraught. His face was red from running and he was gasping and wheezing.

'Calm down,' she said, even though her own heart was thudding. 'Get your breath back, so you can tell us properly.'

Harvey flopped down on to the bed, panting desperately. The moment he could speak, he launched into a great flood of words.

'It's Mum! She went to tell Claudia you had to come home . . . and there was an e-mail saying we had to go to the AIU . . . but there was nobody there, only a voice . . . and it's got Mum and she's just sitting in a chair as if her mind's gone or something . . . and I saw the Headmaster go back in . . . and Mum's there—' He stopped for another gasp of air.

Dinah and Michael looked at each other.

DiBrAc, Dinah thought, with a terrible shuddering of her heart. She dropped on to her knees beside Harvey.

'You think Mum's had something done to her?'

Harvey's face twisted. 'It's horrible. I couldn't make her speak to me, and the voice kept saying: *You're* not clever enough to solve this, Harvey Hunter. *You're* not clever enough to rescue your mother. That's why I came to get you. I thought—'

So that's it, Dinah thought. *That's what I have to do*. She closed her eyes for a second and then stood up. Perfectly calm.

'I'll have to go to the AIU,' she said.

'But you can't!' Lloyd stared at her. 'Didn't you hear what Harvey said? The Headmaster's in there. It must be a trap!'

'I know!' Dinah said fiercely. 'But what else can I do?'

'You won't help by walking straight into the Headmaster's clutches. You know he's trying to catch you! He sent Claudia after you when he saw your face in her badge. He tried to catch you by

157

fixing *Your Wildest Dreams*. And this is his next plan.'

'But—'

Dinah made herself stop. Quarrelling with Lloyd wasn't going to do any good. She had to *think*.

'We must get the Headmaster out of the AIU,' she said slowly.

Lloyd nodded. 'That's sensible. But how?'

'I know!' Michael jumped up excitedly. 'Dinah could walk past one of those peculiar students, with the badges. Then the Headmaster would see her and come out to chase her—'

'And he'd probably catch her,' Lloyd said. 'That wouldn't help.'

'Not if . . . she wasn't really there,' Harvey said. He'd got his breath back now, and he was working something out. 'Suppose *we* trick *him*. There's that badge that Dinah and Ian got at the Outdoor Centre. If one of us put that on—'

'Brilliant!' Dinah beamed at him.

Lloyd nodded. 'Well done, Harvey.' He unzipped his jacket and took out the CB radio. 'I'll get Ian to bring it. Hello? Hello?'

Ian's voice came crackling out of the radio. 'SPLATweb here!'

'It's Lloyd. Is everything OK?'

'Incredible! We've got messages pouring in.' Ian sounded amazed. 'We've just had a letter delivered by motorbike. And someone in that big block of flats is passing on semaphore messages. And there's a pigeon as well. How about you?'

'We've got . . . a problem,' Lloyd said cautiously. He didn't think the Headmaster could possibly be eavesdropping on their call, but he wasn't taking any risks. 'We need the . . . er . . . the emerald fist thing that Plum and Jelly gave you.'

'The emerald—?' For a second, Ian didn't get it. Then he laughed. 'OK. Where are you?'

Lloyd hesitated. Dinah saw that he couldn't think of a nonsense way to explain.

'In the lost scientist's den,' she hissed.

Lloyd grinned and passed it on. 'We're lurking in the lost scientist's den.'

'I'll be right over!' Ian said.

It took him half an hour. By that time, they had the whole plan worked out and Lloyd explained it, pointing out the places on a plan of the university.

Ian looked at Dinah. 'Are you sure you want to do this? It's pretty dangerous.'

'It's just as dangerous for all of you,' Dinah said.

Harvey nodded. 'We're all in it together. SPLAT for ever!'

159

'OK, then.' Ian picked up the plan, looked at it one last time and folded it up. 'Let's get going.'

They crept down to the front door and peered out. The campus was crowded, but there was no sign of any of the weird students. Ian held out his waterproof, with the Green Hand badge rolled inside, and Lloyd took it. He put his finger to his lips.

'Total silence now. Don't let the Headmaster hear anything except what we want him to hear.'

Carefully, he unrolled the waterproof and took out the badge. Keeping it covered with his hand, he pinned it on to Ian's sweatshirt. He looked round, to make sure the others were all out of view, and then dodged out of the way himself.

Right? he mouthed at Dinah.

She nodded. Deliberately, she stepped in front of Ian and began to walk away from him, towards the main road. When she was about fifty metres away, Harvey shouted. 'Hey! Dinah Hunter! Stop!'

Dinah turned to look back, staring straight at the badge on Ian's sweatshirt. Giving it a good view of her face.

'Stop!' Harvey yelled again. 'Come back!'

He dodged in front of Ian and Dinah raced away, round the side of a building. Harvey started after her, with Ian following. The two boys ran between the buildings, twisting and turning, as if Dinah were just ahead of them.

But she wasn't. She ran right round the first building and came back to Lloyd's side.

'Great!' he said. He nodded at Michael. 'Off you go. You've got to meet the others up by the bus stop.'

Michael ran off, and Lloyd grinned at Dinah. 'That was perfect. Let's get up to the AIU and see if it tricked the Headmaster. Is there somewhere we can hide?'

'There's a little garden.' Dinah led the way. 'We can watch from there.'

They didn't have long to wait. They had barely reached the garden when three of the weird students came hurrying out of the AIU. They ran off towards the main road.

Lloyd looked down at his watch and grinned at Dinah. 'Brilliant. The Headmaster's sent them to catch you up by the bus stop. Harvey should be ready to distract them. And Michael and Ian ought to be on the bus by now.'

'If it wasn't late,' Dinah said. She was frowning.

'Don't *worry*.'

'But suppose they catch Harvey—?'

Lloyd grinned. 'They won't even see him. He's brilliant at dodging. They'll just hear him calling your name, leading them on a wild goose chase.'

161

Dinah bit her lip and looked down at the AIU. She wished she could be as confident as Lloyd.

He was checking his watch again. 'Michael and Ian will be jumping *off* the bus now. It only takes a couple of minutes to get to the other end of the university. Michael will be pinning the badge on, and Ian will be shouting your name. The Headmaster should send someone else out in around thirty seconds. Twenty. Ten——'

It went like clockwork. As Lloyd's countdown finished, Claudia came running out of the building. Without hesitating, she headed for the far end of the university.

Miserably, Dinah stared after her. 'She's going to try and catch me.'

'It's not her fault,' Lloyd said. 'It's the Headmaster. And we're going to stop him. Right?'

'Right,' Dinah said.

But inside her head she added, *I hope*. They were all concentrating on getting her into the AIU, as if she would magically solve everything once she was inside. But what was she going to do?

Lloyd was still checking the time.

'OK. Ian's doing the dodging and shouting now. He'll keep Claudia busy. And Michael's racing off to the Sports Centre. If we're lucky, we might see him. Watch that gap between the buildings.'

162

He pointed and Dinah held her breath. She couldn't believe the plan would work so exactly.

But it did. For a split second, they saw Michael in the distance, racing across the opposite slope that led up to the Sports Centre. He disappeared round the side of the Centre, and Lloyd started working things out again.

'He'll have to find somewhere to prop the badge. Then he'll get in front of it and start calling you. And then—'

It could only have taken two or three minutes, but it seemed like hours. Dinah's fists were screwed up tight, and her brain was whirring, thinking of all the things that could go wrong.

Then Lloyd caught his breath.

'There he is,' he said softly.

The Headmaster was standing in the doorway of the AIU.

Until that moment, Dinah hadn't quite believed that it was him. She'd worked it out, logically, but that was quite different from seeing him actually standing there, real and solid.

Exactly the same.

The moment she saw that cold, stern face, she stopped worrying about the things that might go wrong. Nothing could be allowed to go wrong. They had to stop the Headmaster from taking over. Because if he got a grip on things he

163

would fill the whole world with his own cruel efficiency.

There would be no room for feelings, or differences, or imagination.

Dinah clenched her fists and began to concentrate on what she might do.

The Headmaster didn't stand in the doorway for long. He glanced up and down the campus once, and then set off towards the Sports Centre.

Lloyd stood up. 'Ready?'

Dinah gave him the best grin she could manage. 'Let's go.'

They ran down the slope towards the AIU. Michael had told them the security code, but they didn't need it. The moment Dinah touched the entry button, the door swung open by itself. She looked at Lloyd and he shrugged.

'The Headmaster must have forgotten to shut it.'

Dinah didn't think he had, but she wasn't going to argue. 'You'll stay here and keep watch?'

Lloyd nodded. 'Good luck.'

Dinah turned and walked into the building. It was very quiet inside. All the doors were open and she could see that the offices were empty. She made straight for the lab. For a second she paused, to catch her breath. Then she opened the door and went in.

Her mother was sitting in an armchair, with her back to the door.

'Mum?' Dinah said.

There was no answer. Slowly, Dinah walked round the chair. Her mother was wearing a strange headband, with lots of equipment fixed to it. And she was staring straight ahead, with unfocused eyes.

'Mum?' Dinah said again.

There was no reaction.

Stepping forward, Dinah caught hold of her arm. It was warm, and her mother was breathing in an easy, relaxed way, but she didn't make any response. She just went on sitting and staring with the same utterly blank expression.

Slowly, Dinah turned and looked round the room. There was no one else there, but she was aware of something. A sort of presence.

'Where are you?' she shouted. '*Who* are you? What do you want?'

The answer came from behind her, in a woman's voice. Smooth and sweet.

'Hello, Dinah Hunter. I've been waiting for you.'

16

'Which Side Are You On, Dinah Hunter?'

Lloyd couldn't understand why Dinah was being so long. Everyone had left the AIU, hadn't they? Why didn't she just bring Mum out, so that they could escape?

He stuck his head inside the building, but he couldn't hear what was happening, even though the door of the lab was ajar. He was on the verge of going after Dinah when there was a crackle from the CB radio in his hand.

'SPLATbase here!' said Ingrid's voice. 'I've just been pecked by a pigeon.'

'Ssh!' Lloyd hissed. 'I can't talk now!'

'But you've got to!' Ingrid said urgently. 'I've got to tell you the message. From the pigeon.'

'But I can't——'

'Listen!' Ingrid began to read, without giving him any more time to protest:

'News from a hacker——Stop the Hand!
'It's got control of all the land!
'Tonight, at midnight, on the hour
'It'll get the army in its power.
'If it controls our fighting men
'No one will defeat it then!'

Lloyd felt his heart thump. 'Do you think it's true? I mean—is the Hyperbrain really taking over the army?'

'Sounds like it,' Ingrid said. Her voice was scared. 'We've got to do something, Lloyd. We've got to stop him—'

'Don't worry,' Lloyd said. 'We will. We—'

He stopped suddenly. He'd been so busy talking to Ingrid that he had forgotten to keep watch. Now it was too late. The Headmaster was striding down the slope from the Sports Centre. And he was dragging Michael with him.

'Emergency!' Lloyd hissed into the radio. 'Keep silence until I call!'

Sliding the aerial down, he slipped the radio into his pocket. It was too late to warn Dinah. It was too late to hide. All he could do was stand there and watch the Headmaster heading towards him.

Michael was looking at him with helpless, terrified eyes—but the Headmaster barely gave him a glance. As he reached the door, he waved impatiently.

'Out of my way, boy!' he snapped.

It was the eeriest moment of Lloyd's life. He was staring straight into the Headmaster's face, straight at the dark glasses that hid those cold, sea-green eyes. He knew that face almost as well as he knew his own. He had even seen it in

167

his dreams. But the Headmaster didn't recognize him.

Putting out an arm, he brushed Lloyd out of the way. 'Take that toy radio somewhere else,' he said.

He pulled Michael into the AIU and pushed at the door to close it behind them. Just in time, Lloyd stuck out his hand. Instead of shutting, the door swung on to his fingers. He hardly noticed the pain. Holding his breath, he crept through the door and slipped into one of the empty offices.

Inside the lab, Dinah was bending over her mother's chair. Suddenly she felt someone watching her and she straightened and spun round.

A figure had appeared on the far side of the lab, in front of the shelves. It was the woman Dinah and Michael had seen before, and she was standing in exactly the same place.

'Who *are* you?' Dinah said. 'What have you done to my mother?'

The woman gave her a long, slow stare. 'Your mother has . . . provided me with information,' she said at last.

'It's DiBrAc, isn't it? You've destroyed her mind.'

'Nothing is destroyed. Your mother's knowledge is here. Safely stored.'

168

The woman gestured towards the shelves behind her, at the Molecular Storage Units. They were heaped up, just as they had been last time Dinah saw them. But, this time, three of them were translucent and glittering.

'Three?' Dinah said softly.

'They hold the knowledge from three human brains. This one—' The woman pointed. '—is Tim Dexter's.'

Dinah caught her breath. 'Where is he? What have you—'

'He is perfectly safe,' the woman said smoothly. 'And his knowledge has been extremely useful. Especially his design for an interface for the Hyperbrain.'

She smiled, a small, strange smile, and Dinah felt her skin prickle.

'What about the others?' she said.

'The next one comes from a meddling student who came asking questions about Tim Dexter.'

'Peter Giles,' Dinah said.

'That is correct. And this—' The woman made a small gesture towards the third cylinder. Dinah had to fight the scream that exploded inside her.

'That's Mum, isn't it? But why did you do it to *her*? She's not a scientist.'

The woman didn't answer directly. 'I know all about you now, Dinah Hunter. I know how you

169

were adopted. I know that you like sausages and hate ravioli. I know the pattern on your pyjamas and the marks on your last school report. I know—'

'You've destroyed my mother's brain for *that*?'

'Your mother's brain is not destroyed. She can have it back whenever you choose. If—'

If.

Of course there was an if. Dinah had known that, all along. This was a trap, and her mother was the bait. It seemed that the Headmaster and this strange woman both wanted something that only she could give them.

She wished she knew what it was.

'If what?' she said.

The woman glided closer. Her feet were eerily silent on the floor. 'I want to know about the man who says he is the master of the Hyperbrain,' she said.

'You want to know about the Headmaster? Is that *all*?' Dinah felt like crying with relief. 'What do you want to know?'

But the woman shook her head. 'Telling is not enough. You might lie. Or forget. The knowledge must go straight from your mind into the mind of the Hyperbrain. Then I can be sure that I have it all.'

Dinah's eyes travelled to the next empty, opaque Molecular Storage Unit, and the woman nodded.

170

'I can see that you are intelligent and well informed. I shall enjoy exploring your mind.' For a second, her eyes flickered hungrily.

Dinah shuddered. 'Why should I let you destroy my brain as well?'

'Your brain will not be destroyed. And I will make a bargain with you. Give me what I want, and I will restore the rest of your knowledge. And your mother's.'

'What about Tim Dexter?' Dinah said quickly. 'And Peter Giles?'

The woman looked surprised. 'Why should you care about them?'

'Because they're people!'

For a moment, the woman hesitated, considering. Then she nodded. 'Give me Direct Access to your brain and I will give you all the used Storage Units, and tell you what to do with them. And where to find the people who provided the information.'

Dinah looked at her mother's blank, unmoving face and knew that she would have to accept the bargain. But . . . she was being offered everything that she asked. What did she know that was worth so much?

The woman was obviously growing impatient, because she began to murmur in her soft, sweet voice. 'Maybe I have miscalculated. I thought you would want to save your mother. But she's not your *real* mother, is she? Why should you risk your life to save her?'

'Of course she's my real mother!' Dinah said fiercely. 'Nobody could be a realer mother than she is to me! Of course I'll take the risk.' She struggled to stay calm and think clearly, but it was hard when the woman knew everything about her. And how to manipulate her.

'What do you want me to do?' she said.

The woman took another silent step towards her. 'You see the headband your mother is wearing? Take it off, and put it on your own head.'

Dinah undid the headband. Her mother didn't seem aware of what was happening, but Dinah did it very gently, trying to send messages through her fingers. *I'm looking after you, Mum. It's going to be all right.*

Trembling slightly, she lifted the headband, put it on her own head and adjusted it to fit. It was studded with tiny magnetic sensors and transdermal conductors and she had a pretty good idea of the way it would access her brain. But how would it channel the information back to the Hyperbrain?

There had to be a connection somewhere, but she couldn't see it.

The woman didn't explain. She simply waited until the headband was fastened. Then she said,

'Let us waste no more time.' She began to move towards Dinah.

But before she was halfway there, the door was flung open and a tall figure came striding into the room, dragging Michael behind him by one hand.

'Stop!' he shouted. 'Don't let her take what you know, Dinah Hunter—or she will rule the world!'

It was the Headmaster.

Defiantly, Dinah spun round to face him. 'Why should I take your side, against her? You want to rule the world as well, don't you?'

The Headmaster didn't answer in words. Instead, he took hold of Michael's shoulders and pushed him forward, straight at the woman.

Michael staggered, reaching out to save himself from falling. Dinah saw his hands touch the woman's arm. But they didn't stop there. They went on moving, as though there was nothing solid in their way. Michael fell forward and for one brief second—impossibly—he and the woman both occupied the same space.

Then he tumbled to his knees, falling right through the woman's body, and sprawled full length on the floor.

'She is not human,' the Headmaster said. 'She is a hologram. Do you want *that* to rule the world?'

The woman stood perfectly still, expressionless. Michael looked up at her, from the floor.

'You're the interface, aren't you?' he said, in an awed, wondering voice. 'The new interface my father designed.'

Gravely, she nodded. 'Tim Dexter's mind was full of useful knowledge,' she said smoothly.

The Headmaster looked triumphantly at Dinah. 'You see? She is an illusion. When you talk to her, you are really talking to the Hyperbrain. A computer with no human feelings. Do you want to give the world to *that*?'

The woman smiled her small, strange smile and glided soundlessly nearer to Dinah. 'Maybe that would be better than giving the world to *him*,' she murmured.

'I—' Dinah didn't know what to say.

The Headmaster didn't give her a chance to think. He stepped closer too. 'You cannot hand over the whole human race to a machine.'

'And you cannot hand it over to a monster,' said the woman. 'What are you going to do, Dinah Hunter?'

'*Me?*' Dinah said. 'What's it got to do with me?'

All at once, the room was very quiet. Even the air seemed to have grown still. Michael lay motionless on the floor. Mrs Hunter sat unmoving in the chair. The Headmaster and the woman both had their eyes fixed on Dinah.

She looked back steadily. 'What do I know

that's so important? Why does the Hyperbrain want *my* knowledge?'

'She doesn't want it for herself,' the Headmaster said impatiently. 'She wants to keep me from getting it. You know the one thing I need to stop her,' the Headmaster said.

'Why do you need anything? I thought you were the Controller of the Hyperbrain.'

'I am. The Hyperbrain is programmed to obey me, and no one else. I am its master.' A faint frown crossed the Headmaster's face. 'But Tim Dexter made a blunder in his programming. To take over, I need two words. Unless I have them, no one will be able to master the Hyperbrain. It will be out of control, and that woman will run the world to satisfy her thirst for knowledge.'

'And what would you do?' Dinah said.

'I would run it sensibly. Efficiently. Without allowing people to ruin it with their stupid wishes.' The Headmaster dropped his voice suddenly. Instead of shouting at Dinah, he started to croon. 'You know me, Dinah Hunter, don't you? You know what I'm like. Tell these other people. Tell them who I am.'

What was he up to? Dinah took a step back, looking warily at him.

'Tell them who I am,' he crooned. 'Tell them my name. What is it, Dinah?'

'Your name?' Dinah blinked. 'What does that prove?'

'Tell them my name . . . '

Michael sat up suddenly. 'No!' he shouted. 'That's it, Dinah! That's what he needs to take over.'

'What?' Dinah blinked.

'It's the security procedure! He made Dad programme the Hyperbrain to obey a single master. But he didn't tell him to suspend the security procedure. The Hyperbrain won't recognize him until he gives his name.'

Suddenly Dinah understood everything. 'He's got the old Headmaster's face—but he hasn't got his memory. So he doesn't know his name!'

'Don't tell him,' said the woman, from halfway across the room. 'If you do, he will take over the Hyperbrain, and rule the world.'

'And if you don't,' shouted the Headmaster, 'the Hyperbrain will rule the world by itself. Which side are you on, Dinah Hunter?'

Helplessly, Dinah looked from the smooth hologram of the woman's head to the Headmaster's pale, stern face.

What on earth am I going to do? she thought.

17

All the Knowledge in the World

Lloyd had crept right up to the door. He watched in horror as Dinah turned towards the Headmaster.

No! he thought. *You can't take his side!*

Then she turned the other way, towards the beautiful, inhuman interface.

No! Not her either!

All the while, the Headmaster's voice was murmuring on and on. 'My name, Dinah Hunter! Tell me my name. My name . . . '

Dinah looked from one to the other, faster and faster. At last, she laughed harshly. 'Your name's . . . Rumpelstiltskin!'

Lloyd knew it was just a desperate, unfunny joke—but the Headmaster obviously didn't. For an instant, a smile of triumph spread across his face.

'Rumpel Stiltskin! My name—'

Then the woman began to rattle out words. Not in her usual sweet, syrupy way, but in a ragged, erratic voice, as though something had disturbed her. 'Rumpelstilt . . . skin is a . . . dwarf in . . . German fairytale . . . not real name . . . nonsense . . . '

Lloyd saw Dinah's face light up, the way it did when she made a wonderful new discovery. Flinging back her head, she began to chant in a loud, cheerful voice.

' 'Twas brillig and the slithy toves
Did gyre and gimble in the wabe,
All mimsy were the borogoves
And the mome raths outgrabe!'

The Headmaster glared at her. 'What are you saying? Why are you wasting time like this—?'

Oh good! thought Lloyd gleefully. *That's upset him. He doesn't like nonsense. He—*

And then he saw the interface, and for a second he forgot all about the Headmaster. Because she was even more disturbed. Behind her, the computer screen was buzzing and flashing, and her body was beginning to shake and judder. The hologram image had started to turn fuzzy.

'Beware the Jabberwock, my son!' Dinah was chanting:

'The jaws that bite, the claws that catch!
Beware the Jub-jub bird—'

All of a sudden, Michael realized what she was trying to do. Jumping to his feet, he began to chant as well.

'As I was going up the stair
I met a man who wasn't there—'

The Headmaster shook his head from side to

178

side, as if he were trying to get rid of the rubbish Michael and Dinah were speaking. And the woman was growing more and more shapeless. Jagged black stripes were shooting across her image, and flashes of green light were exploding from her shoulders.

It was the nonsense! The Hyperbrain couldn't cope with jokes and nonsense! Lloyd felt like shouting and cheering, but there wasn't time for that yet. Stepping away from the lab doorway, he flicked on the CB radio.

'Calling SPLATweb! Calling SPLATweb! Everyone who's near a Green Hand badge must talk rubbish to it! TALK NONSENSE NOW!'

Mandy stood in the internet café and stared at her CB radio. What was going on? Had Lloyd gone mad?

Ingrid reacted faster. 'Let me have the keyboard, Kate! And you and Mandy send out this message every way you can! Get the pigeons going! Catch the milkman! *Anything!*'

She began to type at top speed, trying to contact anyone who could still get Crazyspace.

They like logic, they like fact,
Fantasy will have them whacked!
Talk rubbish no one understands

179

To all those grabby greenish hands!
Give them nonsense overload!
Chatter junk till they explode!

Mandy understood now. She began to scribble messages on little pieces of paper, fixing them into rings for the pigeons' legs . . . *Talk rubbish no one understands* . . .

Kate was up at the window with a mirror, signalling for all she was worth. Sending out the message to Mirror One, so that it could flash on to Mirror Two and Mirror Three . . . *Give them nonsense overload* . . .

Back in the lab, Dinah still thought she was on her own, except for Michael. She was racking her brains to keep up a constant stream of gibberish.

'One fine day in the middle of the night,
Two dead men got up to fight . . . '

She couldn't concentrate properly, because she knew the Headmaster wouldn't let himself be defeated that easily. He was bound to try something—

'Back to back they faced each other . . . '

She was right. Just as she was searching for the next line, his hand went up to his dark glasses. *No!* she thought. Backing away, she screwed up her eyes to stop herself from seeing those strange green eyes. She heard him chanting as he pulled off the glasses.

'Why are you talking when you are so sleepy, Dinah Hunter? So very, very sleepy . . . '

I'm not sleepy! I'm not! She raised her voice and went on shouting, with her eyes tightly closed.

'And with their swords they shot one another!'

But she couldn't keep her eyes shut. There was a sudden shriek from Michael.

'Dinah! Watch out behind you!'

Whisking round, she saw the hologram woman gliding towards her. She hardly looked human now. Her shape was blurred and jagged and whole sections of her body were breaking down into patterns of swirling dots. But her hands were still the shape they should have been, and they were stretching out towards Dinah. Reaching for her head. Big square hands, with long green fingers reaching out to grab. Once she had the knowledge from Dinah's brain, she would never let it go.

Dinah didn't wait to work out what a hologram could do to her. Instinctively she dodged sideways, spinning away.

And she found herself looking at the Headmaster again.

'You are very sleepy . . . ' he was crooning.

She had never felt so lonely and desperate in her life.

* * *

But she wasn't alone. All over the country, children were getting the message. Gazing at flashing mirrors. Pulling pieces of paper from their pigeons' legs.

They like logic, they like fact,
Fantasy will have them whacked!

People who lived on hills were signalling with flags and boys and girls in the streets were banging on doors and shouting to their friends.

Talk rubbish no one understands
To all those grabby greenish hands!

SPLATweb was working at full stretch. Everywhere people were running towards the nearest Green Hand badge as they deciphered Ingrid's rap.

Give them nonsense overload!
Chatter junk till they explode!

'Squeeble greezzerpop!' Dinah shouted, with her hands over her face. 'Criadion boogledrip!'

She had got beyond remembering nonsense rhymes. And she didn't dare look up because, if she did, the Headmaster would hypnotize her and find out his name. She mustn't let him get it.

'Poodle-noodle farby jerrup! Fiddle-diddle hay-rake!'

182

Somewhere very close, Michael was shouting too, and she could tell that he was near the end of his tether as well.

'Grass is kinder than a horse is blue. How Thursday are you, my dear soup? No pale is motorbike mania.'

The nonsense was disrupting the Hyperbrain. Dinah could hear the computer struggling and buzzing—but it was still going. She and Michael couldn't produce enough nonsense on their own.

'Di!' It was Lloyd's voice, from the doorway. 'Watch out! That woman—'

Frantically, Dinah opened her eyes and spun round. But she was too late. The woman was there, close enough to touch her. Her whole shape was juddering and disintegrating, but her arms were reaching up, up towards Dinah's head. And those horrible green hands were closing round the headband. Grabbing for knowledge.

Dinah had one last moment of clear thinking. *So that's how it's done! There's a force field round the hologram that makes the connection—*

Then the green hands reached the headband she was wearing, and something caught hold of her brain, squeezing it into unconsciousness . . .

'No!' shouted Lloyd. 'Let her go! You can't—'

He ran into the room, but before he was halfway to Dinah he saw the Headmaster's scornful face.

'You fool!' the Headmaster said coldly. 'If you interrupt the DiBrAc process, she will die.'

'But we can't—'

'We can do nothing. The Hyperbrain will not stop now until her mind has gone. Until she is like Tim Dexter and that woman in the chair.'

'But the woman promised she would be all right!' Lloyd said frantically.

The Headmaster looked even more scornful. 'Why should anyone keep a promise?'

Desperately, Lloyd looked at Dinah's blank, white face, trapped between those clutching green hands. It looked small and empty. What could he do? There must be something!

Like magic, a voice spoke out of the air.

Twinkle twinkle little bat!

'What?' The Headmaster frowned and looked round.

How I wonder what you're at, the voice went on cheerfully.

Up above the world so high—

Before it could finish the line, it was joined by another voice.

Far and few, far and few
Are the lands where the Jumblies live—

'What?' said the Headmaster again. 'Who?'

And another.

Little Nanny Etticoat
In a white petticoat—

The woman's glittering hands began to shake and tremble. Suddenly—gloriously—Lloyd knew what they were hearing. It was SPLATweb!

Children all over the country were talking nonsense into Green Hand badges, and their voices were being relayed through the Hyperbrain. The woman was getting the full blast of it. She lost colour completely, so that she became a trembling black shape.

And Dinah's closed eyes opened wide.

'Hold on, Di!' Lloyd yelled. 'It's going to be all right!'

But Dinah wasn't smiling. Her eyes opened wider still. And suddenly she was shouting.

'It's gone into reverse! All the knowledge is coming *into* my brain! It's . . . it's—'

Good? Bad? Looking at her twisted face, Lloyd couldn't tell.

But the Headmaster jumped forward, with a shout of fury. 'You? *You* are getting all the world's knowledge? Give me that headband!'

'You don't . . . understand . . . ' Dinah gasped. 'It's not—'

He didn't listen. Plunging his arms full into the black turmoil of the hologram woman's hands, he

185

pulled at the headband, wrenching it off Dinah's head. She staggered forward, stumbling against Lloyd and Michael.

The Headmaster jammed the headband on to his own head and, for a moment, his eyes glowed with triumph.

'Knowledge is power! All the knowledge in the world will be mine!'

Then a fresh surge of nonsense billowed out of the loudspeakers, as dozens more voices joined in.

Doctor Foster went to Gloucester . . .

Purple rabbit, purple rabbit, catch me if you can . . .

High over Colchester the moon eats chips . . .

Lloyd didn't recognize any of the voices, but Dinah did. She spun round, joyfully. 'Plum!' she shouted. 'Jelly!'

It sounded like more nonsense. For the Hyperbrain, it was obviously the last straw. With a terrible shriek, the woman exploded into a million emerald stars. The computer screen went blank, and the Headmaster crumpled and fell to the ground.

The lab was eerily, abruptly silent.

The silence was broken by the sound of feet running into the building. Ian and Harvey pushed open the lab door.

'What's going on?' Ian said.

'What's happening to Mum?' said Harvey.

186

Dinah bent down and unstrapped the headband from the Headmaster's head. Then she walked over to the shelves on the far side of the lab and took down three glittering cylinders. When she turned round, Lloyd could see that she was exhausted, but she didn't falter.

'It's going to be all right,' she said wearily. 'I know exactly what to do. And I know where your father is, Michael. And Peter Giles. Someone go and phone for an ambulance for the Headmaster, and then I'll start.'

'What I want to know,' said Ingrid, 'is what it was *like*. Having all the knowledge in the world flooding into your head.' She took a large bite of her cream bun.

Dinah looked round the university library, where they were standing. It was crowded with people who'd come to celebrate the re-opening, but she wasn't looking at them. She waved her hand at the shelves full of books.

'Imagine someone trying to squash all that into your head, in twenty seconds.'

Mandy shuddered. 'If the Headmaster hadn't snatched that headband, you'd probably be in a coma in hospital, like him. Knowledge is wonderful, but you can't keep it *all* in your head.'

'Well, you got the right bits,' Lloyd said. 'If the Hyperbrain hadn't gone into reverse, you'd never have found out how to get Mum back to normal.' He glanced across the library, to where Mrs Hunter was chatting to Tim Dexter. 'Do you think they realize what happened?'

Michael shook his head. 'Dad thinks he was ill for a bit. And your mum told me she dropped off to sleep. Dad's already trying to redesign the Hyperbrain so it doesn't overload again. He had a long talk to Mr Smith about it yesterday.'

Lloyd frowned. 'Mr Smith.' He looked across at the man in the brown anorak who had just joined Tim Dexter and Mrs Hunter. 'Of course! He's in Intelligence, isn't he?'

'Artificial Intelligence?' said Mandy.

Lloyd shook his head. 'Spies and stuff, I think.'

Ian whistled. 'And even *he* got hypnotized by the Headmaster? It's frightening, isn't it?'

'No, it's not,' Ingrid said cheerfully. 'Because *we beat the Headmaster*! Mr Smith ought to be grateful to us. I'm going to go and ask him about spying.'

She bounded forward and the others raced after her, to make sure she didn't say anything terrible.

Dinah was left on her own. She stood for a moment, staring round at the library. It was safe now. Like the newspapers and the internet and

188

everything else. For a moment she wondered what life would have been like if they hadn't defeated the Headmaster. And the Hyperbrain.

Then Claudia came over from the other side of the library, and greeted her with a warm, happy smile.

'Dinah! Just the person I wanted to see. I've had a brilliant new thought about that creeper . . . '

She started explaining it, and Dinah forgot all about the Headmaster.

Everyone forgot him, except the nurse who was sitting beside his bed, in Intensive Care.

Waiting to see if his eyes would open . . .

It's not over yet . . .

FACING **THE DEMON HEADMASTER**

'A BRILLIANT SPOOKY SERIES'
Lovereading4kids.co.uk

gillian cross
WINNER OF THE CARNEGIE MEDAL

ISBN 978-0-19-275587-2

'Don't you get it?' Lloyd said. 'He hypnotized her.
It's the Headmaster!'

Purple is the best club *ever*. Everyone loves
DJ Pardoman, but why does he wear a mask?
And what's *really* beneath it?

When Dinah makes a shocking discovery on the
internet, the mystery deepens. And the clues point
to the Demon Headmaster . . .

Can Dinah and her friends stop him this time,
or will the Demon Headmaster triumph with his
most threatening plan yet?